James Hurnard

James Hurnard a Memoir

Chiefly aAutobiographical, with Selections from his Poems

James Hurnard

James Hurnard a Memoir
Chiefly aAutobiographical, with Selections from his Poems

ISBN/EAN: 9783744765213

Printed in Europe, USA, Canada, Australia, Japan

Cover: Foto ©Raphael Reischuk / pixelio.de

More available books at **www.hansebooks.com**

JAMES HURNARD.

A Memoir

CHIEFLY AUTOBIOGRAPHICAL,

WITH

SELECTIONS FROM HIS POEMS.

EDITED BY

HIS WIDOW.

LONDON:

S A M U E L   H A R R I S   &   C O.,

5, BISHOPSGATE WITHOUT, E.C.

1883.

LONDON:

BARRETT, SONS AND CO., PRINTERS,

10, BEER LANE, E.C.

CONTENTS.

―――•○⚬○•―――

CHAPTER I.

EDITOR'S PREFACE.

——••°•°•°°——

IT may require some apology in bringing before the public the Memoirs of one who, though known to a large circle of friends, was not a public character; but I hope the work, which is chiefly in his own words, with occasional alterations, will be found interesting, giving a picture of emigrant life early in this century, and, later on, of quiet useful home life, in which his filial devotion has left a bright example. Amongst his poems, it is believed, will be found some of considerable beauty and high poetic finish.

The compilation having been carried on chiefly upon an invalid couch, the work may, I hope, claim a lenient reception.

LOUISA B. HURNARD.

Lexden, Colchester,
  Fifth Month 10th, 1883.

AUTOBIOGRAPHICAL PREFACE.

Fourth Month 20th, 1837.

BIOGRAPHY has always appeared to me the most delightful department of literature. We naturally take a pleasure in tracing the career of illustrious individuals who have worked their way from obscurity to high honours and distinctions.

Even in those cases where merit has lived and died unrewarded, our interest is but the more excited. Our sympathies are called into activity by misfortunes which could not be averted, by sufferings which did not seem to be deserved, by the rebuffs which the proud have inflicted on those whom they deemed their inferiors, and by the ridicule which little-minded people have bestowed on those whom they could not appreciate.

Whether we read the biographies of princes, statesmen, warriors, poets, or philosophers, we delight, not only in contemplating the splendour of their performances, but in observing the progress of their minds, and the development of their characters.

This feeling of interest is not confined exclusively to the biographies of *great* men. On the contrary, however humble the condition and circumstances of an individual may have been, if the events of his life are well narrated, the workings of his mind clearly described, and the contrasts of his character faithfully pictured, the attention of the reader is sure to be arrested by his story. I hold the opinion that the life of any human being would be interesting if it were well told. Everyone has his hopes and fears, his loves and dislikes, his joys and sorrows, his aspirations and depressions, his recollections of the past and his anticipations of the future; these, like the summer evening clouds on the western horizon, produce an endless variety of novel combinations which fix the attention, enrich the mind, and delight the fancy.

Biography is not only pleasing, but it is eminently instructive. That which Burke says of history may be equally well applied to biography. "In history," said he, "a great volume is unrolled for our instruction, drawing the materials of future wisdom from the past errors and infirmities of mankind." Human life is laid open in biography, and we are taught circumspection by the " past errors and infirmities " of those who have gone before us. Experience is the most expensive thing in the world, and it is always the best policy to borrow that of other people !

Biography may be divided into two kinds—one in which a man relates his own story, and the other in which it is related by some one else.

Each kind has its peculiar advantages. If I write the life of another person I may say many highly interesting things of him which he himself could not mention without subjecting himself to the charge of egotism. At the same time, I labour under a variety of difficulties; I cannot always trace those workings of the mind from which his actions have resulted; there are many things which I cannot fully explain respecting him; and above all, there are many pleasing circumstances in his life of which I have no knowledge, and which are, therefore, irretrievably lost to posterity. On the other hand, if a man writes his own life he enjoys the advantage of having a perfect knowledge of his subject. He can describe the gradual development of his mind, and can trace effects to their remote and secret causes. He best can reveal the hopes that have cheered him, and the sorrows that have depressed him, and describe the struggles of conflicting principles which have agitated his bosom. On the whole, therefore, I am inclined to think that the narrative which a man gives of himself is the most valuable kind of biography. Nor are we to suppose that his account of himself is less authentic than if it had been written by some one else.

JAMES HURNARD:

A Memoir.

———o⊶⊷o———

CHAPTER I.

My ancestors—My birth and early life.

I WAS born at Boreham, a little village near Chelmsford, in Essex, on the 3rd of Third Month, in the year 1808.

Before I proceed with the narrative of my life, I must premise that it is so interwoven with the history of my father's family that I am compelled, in the first place, to devote a few pages to that subject. My great-grandfather was the captain of a vessel. He was, I believe, a man of intemperate habits, and had lowered his condition in society. He left his children in extreme poverty at his death.

His two sons, Robert and John, found themselves, at an early age, turned out into the world to gain a livelihood. These two boys proved themselves to be no common characters. Whether their father, aware that his example was not good, gave them "precept" instead, I know not; but certain it is they possessed three of the most needful qualifications for making

their way in the world—honesty, industry, and fru-
gality. Their first employment was that of farmers'
boys.

One of them, I know not which, used to allow
himself eightpence a year for pocket-money; and one
year contrived to save fourpence out of it.

Of the career of Robert I have learned but little.
He became a respectable farmer, at Latchingdon, in
Essex, remained a single man, prided himself on his
team of fine, fat, coal-black horses, and practised the
easy country hospitality of former times. Of his
brother John, who was my grandfather, I have heard
more particulars.

He was born about the year 1726—I think, at
Manningtree, or some village in the neighbourhood.

Having obtained a situation with a surgeon, at Ford-
ham, near Colchester, he acquired a little knowledge
of medicine, and learned to draw teeth and to bleed.

In process of time John went into the employment
of a shopkeeper at Chelmsford, who was a member of
the Society of Friends. He subsequently became
convinced of the truth of the principles of that Society,
and was received into membership.

About this time he married, and entered into business on his own account as a shopkeeper, in the
village of Springfield. His wife did not live long;
she left a daughter, who was named Jane.

After some little time he married again. The name
of his second wife was Jane Pullyn. Her father and
mother lived at Hellesdon Hall, beyond Norwich, and
had a family, I think, of fourteen children, several
of whom lived to a remarkably great age. When

Jane Pullyn's father died, he left his widow with eleven children. The family soon afterwards were dispersed, and Jane obtained a situation as a shop-maid, I believe, with an aunt.

She subsequently obtained two other situations. I have heard that she stayed seven years at each place, had seven pounds a year at each, and did not take her wages each time until she left. She was, therefore, at a mature age when my grand-father married her. I know not in what year my grandparents moved to the sequestered little village of Boreham. The shop into which they moved was the only one in the place, and was the one in which the bride had passed the last seven years of her service. She lived there while it was in the occupation of John Griffiths, an eminent minister in the Society of Friends. I love to think of that house, and conjure up its picture in my imagi-nation, for under its roof I was born, and my father before me. At this abode John Hurnard continued to reside for the remainer of his days. His business, though small, was profitable; and, if he did not grow rich, he enjoyed a plain abundance. He brought up his family in all the strictness of the religious sect to which he belonged; and such was his cha-racter for benevolence and integrity that few in his circumstances and station in society have acquired a higher or more general respect.

He was an uneducated man; but possessed a sound understanding and a considerable share of wit. But it was in conversation and in the relation of anecdotes that he especially excelled. Of anecdotes he possessed an inexhaustible store ; and when he related them in his slow impressive manner there was something about him that fixed the attention of his listeners.

He was distinguished by great personal courage and firmness of character; and the following incident will show that he was not deficient in presence of mind.

He happened to be in London during the riots in the time of Wilkes, the great popular demagogue. The streets were deserted except by the inflamed mob who paraded them in lawless triumph, and everything wore the aspect of anarchy.

John Hurnard, not troubling himself about political affairs, proceeded, in his usual way, to attend to the business that called him to London. He crossed London Bridge, but not another person was to be seen upon it. While passing, however, along Tooley Street, he suddenly beheld the mob at a short distance advancing towards him. What was to be done? To go forward seemed impossible; and to attempt to escape equally dangerous, for the populace had shot a young man the same day who had run away from them.

Dressed in his plain attire therefore, and consequently presenting a somewhat striking appearance, he boldly walked towards the dense mass of people whom he saw approaching. On coming up to them he took off his hat, and, waving it in the air, shouted at the top of his voice, " Wilkes for ever ! " At once the mob, dividing on each hand, made a way for him to pass through the midst of them ; and, waving their hats, responded to his words, and rent the air with shouts of " Wilkes for ever ! "

I shall frequently have occasion, in the succeeding pages, to advert to my grandfather ; but there is one other anecdote of him which I think it well to insert here. I requested my father, some time ago, to write it down for me. He complied with my request. I shall, therefore, give it in his own words :—

" I think it was about the year 1790 that my father was applied to on behalf of a man who had been in the Excise, and who, for some fraud which he had committed, was then immured in Chelmsford gaol, where he had been confined for the said offence about three years without a prospect of liberation, except in the event of the King's death, when a gaol delivery takes place of persons in confinement for such offences.

" This man, having heard the character of my father, sent a respectful message requesting to see him. He went to him accordingly, heard his statement of facts as to the length of time that he had been in prison ; the situation of his suffering family, consisting, I think, of a wife and several children ; and wished to know how he could serve him. He requested that my father would be so kind as to speak to one of the Commissioners of the Board of Excise, who, he thought, could, if he pleased, procure his release. My father undertook this delicate and difficult task, which few in his station who knew the character of this Commissioner would have dared to undertake, or could have hoped to succeed in. He resided part of the week in London, and the other part at his mansion, New Hall, Boreham. He was of an over-bearing, dictatorial, and passionate temper, and could ill brook control, especially from an inferior. But these were not qualities to daunt an honest Friend in the discharge of what he believed to be his duty, namely, to serve a fellow-creature in distress. He therefore soon waited upon the Commissioner, and, on being announced, was ushered into the presence of the great man, who addressed my father thus : ' Sit down, friend. What is your business with me ? '

" ' I have some business with thee,' said my father; ' but before I mention it I will, if thee please, take a piece of bread and cheese after my walk.'

" ' So you shall, friend,' said the other, and immediately rang the bell, and ordered some cold meat and bread and cheese to be set on the table, and while my father was eating they chatted on indifferent subjects. As soon as he had done, the gentleman, impatient to know his errand, again said, ' Well, now, friend, what is your business ? '

" ' I am come,' said my father, ' to intercede with thee on behalf of a poor man now suffering imprisonment for a fraud committed against the Excise Laws, and I believe it is in thy power to procure his release.'

" ' What is his name ? ' he asked.

" My father had no sooner mentioned the name than he gave way to the most violent and unrestrained expressions of anger imaginable, till he actually frothed at the mouth with passion, swearing he should ' lie in gaol and rot ; which he well deserved.'

" My father sat silent, not attempting to speak till the ebullition of his wrath began to subside ; he then mildly said he did not come there to extenuate the man's crime, but would put to his consideration whether a confinement in gaol of three years' duration was not a sufficient punishment for his offence; and I believe he also appealed to him on behalf of the man's wife and children.

"His simple advocacy found its way to the heart of the great man and disarmed him of his anger, and he said, 'Well, I will do what I can for you.'

"'But what further steps must I take in the case?' asked my father.

"'Why,' said he, 'go to the man and tell him to draw up a petition to the Board.'

"'And will thee present it?' said my father.

"He promised that he would; and they parted in a very friendly manner. The result was that in three weeks the prisoner was set at liberty; and I remember his coming over to thank my father for his kindness."

While the great ones of the world delight to point to the long line of their ancestors, too often distinguished more by their titles than by their worth, I ask no one's leave while I thus linger over these anecdotes of my own upright and independent forefather. If the titled are proud of their ancestors, I, too, according to my notion of human excellence, have a right to be proud of mine.

It was in the year 1795 that John Hurnard was taken ill as he was going up to London in the coach. He reached his destination, but survived only a few days, leaving a wife, two sons, and two married daughters, namely, John, Rebecca, Mary, and Robert.

His daughter Rebecca married John Steed, of Earith, in Huntingdonshire; and Mary married Thomas Docwra, of Latchingdon. Robert was my father. He was born in 1774, and was sent to Ackworth School at an early age. This school was a newly-established one, and belonged to the Society of Friends.

But the period at length arrived when he was to enter on the cares of life; for his father died, and at the age of twenty-one he succeeded him in his business.

My grandfather had not accumulated what is termed wealth, but he had a sufficiency for his wants; such was the unanxious way in which he lived that I have heard he never took stock. His mode of living was simple, and trade was less of a struggle then than it has been since.

There is another subject to which I must here advert. My father, early in life, began to feel the importance of education. He possessed a taste for literature; and he industriously set about the task of self-improvement. He read a great deal, and took lessons in French of one of the poor priests whom the Revolution had exiled from France. He also cultivated the acquaintance of educated persons, and, as he inherited considerable talents for conversation, he soon outshone the other members of his family.

My father, at his outset in life, like my uncle John, underwent a severe stroke of affliction. The young woman to whom he was engaged was taken ill and died. He was young, and his loss deeply afflicted him. He had, however, an uncle, Matthew Fennell, of Bury, in Suffolk, a worthy man, who some time afterwards strenuously recommended him to come and see a young woman of the name of Hannah Clark, who was residing with a brother in that town. My father at first was in no mood to undertake such an enterprise. His indefatigable uncle, however, introduced him to the young woman ; he was pleased with her, paid his addresses to her, and at length obtained his suit.

Hannah Clark was born at Chipping Norton, in Oxfordshire, in the year 1767. She was the daughter of John and Hannah Clark. Her father, I have heard, was a useful man in his day, and did good service by his exertions to prevent the enclosure of Chipping Norton Common. His wife was an amiable woman, of considerable talent and great beauty. He died young, leaving a large family, and his wife survived his loss only about three months.

Their youngest son was Bracy Clark, whose name is not unknown in the scientific world (he was a noted veterinary surgeon) ; their fourth daughter was my mother.

Bereft of their parents at an early age, inheriting some property, and possessing talents and personal attractions, the family were much exposed to the contact of the world, and they preserved but little appearance of being members of the Society in which they had been born. My mother, however, at length formed a friendship with a young woman of remarkable piety who was in membership, and her example had a great effect in attaching her to the Society of Friends. I have heard that my mother had many suitors; and as she was brought up a lady and had a fortune of a thousand pounds, it was rather remarkable that she should accept my father, who was then a bashful young man, and not much refined in his manners by polished society. But my mother was a woman of a calm and unambitious character, and possessed a discerning mind; and she appreciated my father's worth as well as his abilities.

Great were the preparations at Boreham to receive the bride.

My grandmother, who had kept my father's house, removed to a cottage at the bottom of the garden.

Alterations were made in the house and premises. The sitting-room, with its nicely sanded floor, was converted into a carpeted parlour, and the house was duly furnished according to more modern notions.

The marriage of my parents took place on the 7th of Tenth Month, 1800.

My father at the time was twenty-six years of age, and my mother thirty-two; and, in the course of the ensuing eight years they had four children, viz., Lucy, William Clark, Ann, and myself.

I have now brought down the history of my family to the time of my birth.

As I have stated before, I was born on the 3rd day of the Third Month in the year 1808. My life, I have heard, was very near being brought to a premature close by an adventure of mine during my infancy. It happened thus :—

My mother went to pay a visit to her brother, John Clark, at Bury, and of course she took me with her. One day I was left in the parlour with no one to take care of me but a negligent girl.

Placed on the floor, and finding myself at liberty, and, moreover, being in a new place, my roving disposition was excited, and I crawled forth to make discoveries.

Meanwhile the girl, having a great many things to think of, very soon forgot all about me. After awhile, however, hearing a noise, she looked round, and, greatly to her alarm, perceived that I had made my way to the fire-place, and crawled completely underneath the grate where a large fire was burning. Happily no sparks fell upon me ; and I was snatched from my perilous situation without sustaining any injury.

I learned my letters by a very simple method long before I learned to talk. My father pasted the letters of the alphabet in large Roman characters on the separate pages of an old book. I was soon taught their names, and learned to turn over the leaves till I found any one that was required.

I remember very well being first sent to school. It was kept in an upstairs room in a house across the Green. The schoolmistress was a little, tidy, old-fashioned woman, who went by the name of Dame Rutley. My terror of her has imprinted her appearance on my mind very distinctly. She used a huge pair of spectacles, through which, she was wont to tell us, she could see us when she was not looking at us. Round her cap she wore a black band, and at her side hung a large, shining pair of scissors, and a great black pincushion. She had seen trouble—but

of that I knew nothing then—and trouble, added to
the wear and tear of human patience, expended in
planting the seeds of knowledge in stubborn ground,
had soured her disposition. She used to box our ears
unmercifully.   I once played truant, and amused
myself much to my satisfaction.   My eldest sister,
however, found me out.   I escaped without punishment, but was sensible that I had done wrong, and
I never played truant again.   There is an indescribable pleasure in looking back on the morning of
life.   When we recur to the years of our childhood,
time seems to sift out the memory of our youthful
sorrows, and preserve nothing but the recollection of
our innocent enjoyments.   My parents, indeed, were
blessed with a happy family circle.   Their children
were trained up in the practice of moral and religious
habits with sedulous anxiety.   We were not allowed
to associate with children in the street, and, being
well-managed and amused at home, we scarcely felt
the restriction.   It was the practice in the family
to have a portion of the Scriptures read every
morning, after 'breakfast, in the presence of the
assembled household.   On a First-day evening some
Friends' book was substituted, perhaps Chalkley's
life, or Woolman's, or Ellwood's — all of them
breathing devoted piety, and rendered interesting by
diversified adventures.   It must not be supposed,
however, that our reading was restricted to Friends'
books.   I well remember listening with delighted
attention while my brother read aloud to my sisters
and me the "Surprising Adventures of Robinson
Crusoe."   In those early years of my life I was a

lively, lighthearted child, but I am not aware that I displayed any appearance of superior talent. My memory was never tenacious, and even then any momentary perturbation would suspend its powers. My peculiar mental constitution has often made me appear a dunce, and, being painfully sensitive of shame, I have suffered accordingly. I was, happily, not subjected to the process of undergoing a premature education, according to the manner of modern times.

How can I describe the delight afforded by one little event of my childhood—a journey to Southend? All of us went, we young ones being packed in the head of the chaise. On beholding the sea my delight was unbounded. That was, indeed, a happy day! My notions of space acquired a new character.

On its unstable waves, with trembling pleasure, and almost overpowered with novelty, I soon had a ride. I little foresaw, while dancing, for the first time, on the green sea, the events of future years.

Of such trifles as these our life is made up.

CHAPTER II.

Removal from Boreham to Kelvedon—School life—Hard
times—Contemplated emigration.

But I must now turn away from the recollection
of my early years, to enter on the important subject
—the affairs of the family.

At the time of my father's marriage, the country
was deeply involved in the calamity of a Continental
war.   Every kind of commodity was enormously dear.
The single circumstance that the price of a quartern
loaf was 1s. 10½d. will give some notion of the state
of the times.   My father at once found that his
domestic expenditure was doubled, and the claims of
an increasing family soon began to be felt.   The
unwelcome truth was forced upon him that, with all
his care, his little property was diminishing.   Year
after year the depressing conviction was brought
home to him that his expenses exceeded his income.
With a beloved companion whose happiness was
identified with his own, and a young family growing
up around him for whom he felt all a parent's love,
the circumstances in which he was placed were
deeply harassing and painful.   His exigencies, at
length, drove him into the dangerous practice of
drawing bills.   This system of conducting business
soon increased his perplexities.   He was continually
in want of money, and this kept him in a state of
mental trepidation and anxiety lest demands should

be made upon him which he would be unable to meet. I have often heard him say that he used sometimes to envy the day labourers who passed his door, exempt, as they appeared, from the cares which surrounded him.

Many were the Providential interpositions which he experienced in those days of tribulation. One little circumstance I must not omit. My father was always remarkably regular in the attendance at his usual place of worship at Chelmsford, though the distance was four miles. One First-day morning the weather was extremely wet and unfavourable for going out. His brother-in-law, Henry Clark, who happened at that time to be on a visit at Boreham, recommended him, therefore, not to go. " Oh, yes, I shall," he replied, " perhaps I may find a fifty-pound note on the road." When he returned his brother-in-law took care to ask him if he had found the fifty-pound note. " No," he replied, with an air of satisfaction, "not a fifty pound note, but a hundred." It appeared that, on entering Chelmsford, a friend had met him with a letter containing the pleasing intelligence that a distant relation had left my mother a legacy of one hundred pounds. I need not say how acceptable it proved.

On the whole the difficulties which he went through were, without doubt, of service in the formation of his religious character; and I believe that he was not insensible that they were intended for his ultimate benefit. About this time my father found out that the field which he had bought contained brick-earth. In the hope of improving his circumstances, without knowing much about the business, he commenced brick-making.

This only served, by engrossing his capital, to increase his difficulties.

Several of his friends, who were millers, appeared to be thriving men; he therefore turned his attention to the milling business.

A mill was to be let about a mile off, at Little Baddow, and he resolved to go and look at it. On entering the mill he was rather startled at seeing an acquaintance of his of the name of Mark Whitehead, who was there on the same errand.

Eventually they went into partnership with each other and hired the mill.

The capital with which my father entered into this engagement was principally lent to him by his brother-in-law, Thomas Docwra, who was descended from an ancient and distinguished line of ancestors.

The following paragraph from the *Morning Chronicle*, in reference to the origin of the Twopenny Post Office, contains some curious particulars respecting the family.

"It is not generally known that this important benefit to the comfort and convenience of the inhabitants of London and its environs, and also to the revenue, believed to be between two thousand and three thousand pounds per annum, was the invention of a Mr. Docwra, who, about the year 1680, seeing the deficiencies in this respect of the General Post, established an office for the conveyance of letters to all parts of London and its environs, within ten miles, at one penny each, purchasing a great number of horses, and engaging steady men, who, it may be supposed, in those times were armed. It almost instantly gained universal approval and acceptance. The Government soon cast an anxious eye on this powerful novelty; and, finally, took it into their own hands.

" What licence or patent he had is not fully known; but it is understood he had some, besides a moral right; but he, imprudently, made no demand for compensation.

" It is a singular fact that to another of the same family, London is indebted for one of its principal ancient relics, viz., St. John's Gate, Clerkenwell, built by Sir Thomas Docwra, the last Grand Prior of Malta in England, who sat in the House of Peers. His family arms, derived from Palestine, are carved on the outside, and painted on the roof.

" This was a noble and very generous family, originally in the north, afterwards in Herts, and in Ireland, where they obtained lands and a peerage for distinguished services in 1621. They were allied to many noble families; and, through that of the first Lord of St. John of Bletso, to the royal stock. Of their name, between 1100 and 1650, they reckoned about twenty knights, English and foreign. A grand memorial is seen in Lilly Church, Herts; and two houses, styled Docwra Hall, remain at Kendal and Penrith."

My father soon found his new business to be liable to serious fluctuations.

At that time the power of Napoleon was flickering like a taper in its socket; and political events affected

the markets in a terrific manner. I have heard my
father say that, on one occasion, he and his partner
bought wheat at thirty-eight pounds and a crown a
load ! and before they could make it into flour they
could buy wheat equally as good at twenty pounds a
load.   These fluctuations were frequently taking
place; the business, therefore, was extremely dangerous except to men of large capital.

At the end of two or three years he determined to
dissolve the partnership, and succeeded in obtaining
another mill about eight miles off, at Kelvedon.

I shall never forget receiving the first intimation
that we were going to leave Boreham. I could point
out the spot, even now, where I stood at the time.
It was like awakening from a long and pleasant
dream. The thought of quitting the place of my
birth had never before crossed my mind. In childhood we have no comprehension of the vicissitudes
of life. We have not lived long enough to notice
the effects which time produces. We take for granted
that the old were always old; and we fancy, though
we ourselves may grow bigger, we shall always still
be young.   The illusion, however, is, at length,
destroyed ; and the price that we pay for the knowledge which we acquire is sorrow of heart.

It was in the year 1815 that we removed to
Kelvedon, into the house at the corner near the
public pump.

Soon after we came to reside at Kelvedon my
brother was sent off to an excellent boarding-school
at Epping. My father set a high value on education ; and, as he never expected to be able to give

his children much property, he determined to give them a good share of knowledge.

My sisters were sent as day-scholars to a superior boarding-school in the village. It was kept by two intelligent ladies of the name of Jane and Elizabeth Cubbidge.

Being too young to go to school, my father, by the aid of a little coercion, made me write copies, and wear out my table book at home. In the science of figures I made extremely small progress. I had, even then, an unconquerable aversion to anything like drudgery. The delight of my boyish days was angling. The river and ponds in the neighbourhood of my father's mill afforded me ample scope for this amusement, and much of my time was spent in it.

In the year that we removed to Kelvedon occurred the far-famed Battle of Waterloo. Many of the troops that were there passed through Kelvedon on their way to the place of embarkation for the Continent. The village was kept in a constant state of excitement by the passing regiments, with their martial music and trains of baggage-waggons. In a few months they returned victorious; but, oh, how changed! Their looks were jaded, their clothes were shabby, and the numbers of wounded men plainly told how dreadful had been the conflict.

I used, sometimes, to accompany my father when he went out into the street to talk to the soldiers, and heard them describe the great battle. I remember one of them said he had been in many engagements before; but they were all child's play compared with it. The circumstances which I have mentioned, together with the great topic of the times, the downfall and flight of Napoleon, all tended to excite my young and susceptible mind.

I shall never forget the pleasant evenings that we used to have at this period of my life. As soon as my father reached his long tobacco-pipe, my sister Ann and I used to sidle up to him, and say, " Do, father, tell us a tale!" "Stop a bit," he would reply, " till I have lighted my pipe ; " and, with that, he would very deliberately begin to fill it with tobacco, little by little, with all the art of a true smoker ; and appeared to be considering what tale to tell us. Meanwhile, we were watching him with eager and impatient countenances, and fancied that he kept us as long as possible in suspense. At length his pipe was filled, and, taking a pipe-light, he would slowly and thoroughly ignite the soothing weed, and not till then would he begin. His tales were sometimes laughable and sometimes serious, but always interesting.

At the commencement of the year 1818, I was sent to a boarding-school, about eight miles distant, at Earl's Colne. It was kept by a minister in the Society of Friends, named William Impey. I was, without doubt, one of the best boys in the school ; and so I ought, for, whatever my natural disposition might be, I had excellent parents to train me up, as the following letter from my father, while I was at school, will evince :—

" Kelvedon, Tenth Month 1st, 1818.

"*. . . . Above all, my dear James, I hope thou art daily endeavouring to be a *good boy;* indeed I cannot suppose thou hast forgotten, or wilt forget, the good advice thy dear mother and I have often given thee, namely, that as we are never for a moment out of the Almighty's sight, so He knows all that we say and do ; and as He loves those who love Him, so they may reasonably expect His blessing who are careful not to offend Him by saying or doing what is amiss, and who strive to be thankful for all His favours. Among so many schoolfellows, there may, perhaps, be some who possibly, may not have had the same watchful care over them which thou hast had, or who may have slighted it ; do thou set them a good example, and never associate or play with a boy who does not fear to tell an untfuth ; and be sure never to vex or tease any, especially those who are less than thyself; and be always willing to forgive those who have offended thee. Thus thou wilt seldom feel uncomfortable in thy mind, and we shall think it a blessing to have such a son.

"I remain,

" Thy affectionate father,

" ROBERT HURNARD."

I insert the above letter as a kind of acknowledgment of my parents' care over me. How well do I remember shedding tears while reading it. In truth I was a tender-hearted child.

To the care of my father and mother, in those days, how much do I owe ! They taught me rather by example than precept, and led me rather than coerced me. I am grateful to them also, for not

weighing down my young spirits with the drudgery
of acquiring unavailable knowledge.

Contrary to what would be the general opinion of
my fellow-men, and what might suit some characters,
I esteem it an advantage to me that circumstances
prevented me from going again to school. If I had
continued there, I should, probably, by tedious
industry, have become technically correct in the
usual branches of education, and then have been
driven forward into the unfathomable bog of Latin
and Greek, where my spirit would have been worn
out, and where, eventually, I should have foundered.
As it was, the world became my school, and in this
school I selected my own teachers and my own
studies. I might lose in point of rudimental accuracy,
but acquired larger views, sounder opinions, and freer
processes of thought, and my knowledge was less
reflected from books than radiated from actual life.

When I stepped once more into our cheerful front
parlour at Kelvedon, how warm was the greeting that
I received !

I had not long returned when my sister Lucy asked
whether anyone had told me where they were going.
I replied in the negative. She then informed me that
we were likely to leave England: that we were going
to emigrate to America ! I was startled at this
intelligence, but not much displeased. The thought
of beholding new sights and scenes found a respon-
sive feeling in my heart; and, if I was not delighted
with the prospect of wandering over sea and land, I
was anything but sorry that I was not to return to
school again.

The general distress of the times had induced many persons about this period to emigrate to America. It occurred to my father to expatriate his family to the back settlements of that country, where, according to popular report, it was less of a struggle to live than in his native land. When my parents contrasted their present difficulties and prospects with the picture which they formed of the happiness of settling down in a new country where the land was cheap, and the soil was rich, and provisions were abundant ; where there were no tithes, no taxes, nor poor-rates ; where there was plenty for the time present, and no anxiety for the future,—they paused— they wavered—they made up their minds to go. This determination, however, was not arrived at without fervent and humble supplications to the Guide of the righteous and the Author of all good to direct their steps aright, and to bless them in the way.

As my father intended to become a farmer in the wilds of Ohio, he resolved to take a youth with him as an assistant in the family. There was a young man in the village, a native of Oxfordshire, who had a brother at home who, he thought, would be glad to go with us. He was accordingly sent for to come on approval. Eventually it was settled that he should accompany us ; and he was regularly bound apprentice to my father to learn whatever business he might engage in. His name was Christopher Stopes. He was about sixteen years of age. His father being a farmer, he had been brought up in a way which seemed to qualify him well to succeed in a new country. At driving a bargain he was cleverer than most men, and felt himself, in short, equal to almost any undertaking.

And now came the busy preparations for our departure; the packing up of three distinct kinds of articles, some to use on board ship, some when we landed, and the others when we were duly settled; and then the sale of the remainder of our goods and chattels.

I must here mention that my uncle, William Clark, who was a tanner at Moulsey, finding that his business did not answer, and having a large family to provide for, had resolved to accompany us. My father and uncle accordingly agreed to take one side of the ship *Thames*, about to sail for New York, for their party consisting of about thirty persons. And now, having sent off our packages to London to be stowed away on board the ship, and having taken an affectionate leave of our relations, friends, and neighbours, and we young ones having received a shower of presents of books, knives, &c., we left Kelvedon by the Coggeshall coach on the morning of the 1st of the Fourth Month, 1819. It was on the 4th of the Fourth Month that we put off from Gravesend in a boat to the vessel, and bade farewell to our native land.

CHAPTER III.

Voyage across the Atlantic—Early adventures before settling.

EVERYTHING around us was new and strange ; and the charm of novelty dispelled the sense of sorrow. On climbing up the side of the ship I seemed to enter a new world, where all was disorder, and the inhabitants of which appeared to be a most motley race of creatures. The anchor, however, was soon weighed, the sails were unfurled, and we glided down the river. It is difficult to describe the scene of confusion which presented itself on going below into the steerage. It seemed almost filled with boxes and packages of various kinds, some of which ought to have been below in the hold ; others, at the same time, which ought to have been left above, were below. Some of the passengers were trying to find their boxes, others were busy nailing up old curtains before their berths, and others preparing their dinners. It was a rich scene of confusion. Among our stores we had a half-hundred of red herrings. They smelt rather strongly, and one of the company proposed to " heave them overboard." Some one of us, however, contrived to put them out of sight, and they proved very acceptable afterwards. Our steerage was 34 feet in length by 24 feet in breadth. Round the sides and further end were two tiers of berths, one above the other, each large enough for two persons to sleep in. Along the middle of the steerage boxes and packages

were piled up almost to the ceiling, filled with stores
for the voyage, belonging to the various passengers.
Our steerage, therefore, was our bedroom, sitting-
room, store-room, and pantry ; and as there were
sixty occupants, the population was rather dense.

For the first few days we were most of us too ill to
go on deck much, or to pay a great deal of attention
to the English coast along which we were sailing.
The night of the 8th was very tempestuous. The
wind howled through the rigging, the waves dashed
over the vessel, and the holloaing of the sailors on
deck increased the terrors of the night. Some of our
timid passengers lay and trembled like mice. Every
now and then a ponderous wave would descend upon
the deck like a cart-load of gravel, while the berths
creaked, the tin-ware rattled, and some of the boxes
getting loose tumbled about the floor of the steerage
in disorder. Life at sea we found to be not altogether
a state of perfect happiness. Sixty of us being cooped
up in one room, which it was impossible to ventilate.
Setting aside sea-sickness, it is no wonder that our
appetites were not very good ; we relished almost
nothing. Potatoes and eggs were our principal food.
While we were in this dainty condition someone
happened to remember our half-hundred of red
herrings. They were soon produced and tasted, and
at once pronounced a great delicacy. Our neighbours
perceived the savoury smell, and soon begged to be
supplied with a few. No one now any longer proposed to " heave them overboard." The demand for
our red herrings increased. The fame of them spread
far and wide, and, at length, reached the cabin. But

the supply was limited, and fast diminishing. Such was the request in which they were held at last, that when the steward of the cabin came a-begging, he confined his request to the favour of half a herring!

The only fireplace on board was in the caboose, or little kitchen on deck. As there were not only the steerage passengers to cook for, but those in the cabin also, as well as the sailors, it may easily be imagined that there was considerable competition for the use of the fireplace. The gentlefolks in the cabin, and the crew of the ship, had everything provided for them by the steward and the cook, but the poor steerage passengers had to fight their own battle, and scramble amongst themselves for precedence.

As my own health had improved, I kept principally on deck, and enjoyed, even thus early in life, the grandeur of ocean scenery, and inhaled the pure air with delight.

What glorious sunsets there are at sea! Not the beams alone, but the broad expanse of water, forming together one grand spectacle, glowing and glittering in the golden effulgence of the setting sun! Not less beautiful were the moonlight nights.

By the 25th we reached the banks of Newfoundland. The scene which this dreary region presented I shall never forget. The weather was boisterous, the sea agitated and turbid, the air piercingly cold, and the horizon contracted by a dull impenetrable fog. One might imagine oneself arrived at the gloomy confines of some unexplored ocean.

The 30th was a fine blowing day. By holding fast I managed to keep my seat on deck in spite of

the tremendous rolls of the ship. While I was
sitting in a mood of idle contemplation someone
espied a vessel on the starboard bow. It had no
sail set and appeared to be rolling about at the
mercy of the wind and waves. The second mate
reached the telescope from the companion-way and,
after looking at the vessel through it for a few
moments, gave it as his opinion that it was in
distress. She was about half a mile off to windward
of us; but no sign of any living creature was to
be seen on board. All eyes were intently turned
towards her when, suddenly, a man appeared on her
deck. It seemed that he saw us, for he instantly
took off his hat and waved it in the air. The effect
upon us was electrical, and we waved our hats
joyfully in reply. He presently disappeared again,
and the next time that the vessel was borne to the
top of the waves we perceived that there were three
others on deck. One of them was seen crawling
along the bowsprit and, in a short time, they contrived
to set their jib-sail. Meanwhile our captain had
given orders to back our own topsails; and the ship
was laid to in order to await the strange vessel
which now drove towards us before the wind. It
was an anxious and exciting interval to us all. As
she approached us we observed the waves every now
and then sweep over her deck like a cascade. But
we were not long kept in suspense. She soon neared
us, and the first words that we heard from her crew
were, " We are going down ! " With considerable
difficulty the poor fellows were got on board our
vessel; their own was then set adrift either to sink

or swim.   The poor men were sickly and half-starved,
and altogether in a wretched plight.

> " Seventy days we have thus been tossed
> In a leaky sloop with our rudder lost;
> Our food was salt beef and Indian corn,
> No water we had, it had long been gone;
> But we spread forth a sheet whene'er it rained,
> And what we wrung out was all we obtained."
>   " *The Sloop in Distress.*"

The 2nd of the Fifth Month was a remarkably
fine day.   We spoke a brig bound to Boston, laden
with dried fruits; eighty-eight days from Trieste,
and forty-nine from Gibraltar.   A little incident of
this kind is a highly interesting event at sea.

On the morning of the 6th several of us, myself
among the number, rose at daybreak in the hope of
seeing land.   We saw the sun rise majestically, but
no land was to be seen.   At nine o'clock, however,
it was discovered right ahead, lying like a dense
cloud along the horizon.   The announcement diffused
universal joy.   The morning was most beautiful,
and we were all in a mood to be happy.   Emotions
of delight warmed and exhilarated every heart.   We
were now soon to escape from our long weary ocean-
imprisonment, and before us lay the land of our
destination—a world both new and strange.   Meanwhile a fresh breeze bore us rapidly forward over the
green sea.   A large number of coasting vessels were
in sight, and a pilot soon boarded us.   Directly in
front was the entrance to the bay of New York,
while to the right stretched Long Island, and, on

the left, the lovely highlands of Neversink, unfolding
fresh beauties the nearer we drew.   We were highly
pleased with the appearance of the country along
which we were sailing.   The scenery was rich, and
every now and then adorned with tasteful villas and
cheerful farmhouses.   But the ship rapidly passed
onward, and, about three o'clock, we cast anchor
off the great commercial city of New York, after a
voyage of thirty-two days.

My brother having boasted one day that he was
the last off English ground, I had predetermined to
be the first who should set foot in America.   I
managed to effect my object, but at the cost of a
reprimand from my father for my precipitancy.

Having taken up our abode in Pearl Street, we
proceeded to clear out our baggage from the ship.
The remainder of our store provisions were sold by
auction for a mere trifle; and our packages were
shipped off to Philadelphia to be put into a warehouse till we should be settled.   The weather set in
wet and cold during this bustling time, and my
sister Lucy was taken ill.   This was an awkward
and distressing circumstance, and occasioned us
some detention.   My uncle, William Clark, took
lodgings for his family at another house.   They left
New York before us, and proceeded to Morris Birk-
beck's settlement in Illinois, where they purchased
land and became farmers.   I may add that, in going
down the river Ohio in an ark, they had the misfortune to lose one of their little girls overboard.
She was a sweet child, and the melancholy event
cast a gloom over their opening career.   Meanwhile

my father and mother made good use of their letters
of introduction, and were handsomely invited and
kindly entertained by several of the opulent in the
city, who were members of the same sect.

During our stay the Yearly Meeting of the Society
took place, and many persons from distant parts
were there. At one table at which my father dined,
he was placed next to a personage who had risen,
at an age beyond the usual term of human life, to
unenviable distinction. This man was Elias Hicks.
He was a minister in the Society who had adopted
Unitarian sentiments. He was a plain country
farmer, extremely simple in his dress, and affable in
his manners. In countenance he bore, it was said,
a strong resemblance to Washington. He was
greatly followed, and collected a large number of
adherents.

Eventually he effected a great and afflictive schism
in the Society, which shook it to its very foundation.
My father had considerable conversation with him
as they sat at dinner, and spoke to him, among other
things, about his preaching, and told him plainly
that if he were to go to England the Elders in
the Society there would not allow him to preach.
" Indeed ! " he retorted, " what would they do to
me ; would they hang me ? " This, doubtless, was a
dexterous allusion to the sanguinary laws of England.
My father told him, in reply, that they would not
hang him, but that they would transport him back
to his own country again. The old man, at parting,
kindly invited my father to visit him at his farm in
Long Island. My father, by thus mixing in society,

acquired a knowledge of the people, and had the advantage of hearing their disinterested opinions with regard to his future movements. His friends, finding him to be a man of a social character, with a gentlewoman for his wife, and having a family of slim delicate-faced children, advised him strenuously to give up his intention of going to settle in the backwoods of the country.

On the 31st of Fifth Month we left New York, having been there upwards of three weeks. After an agreeable journey we reached the beautiful city of Philadelphia. There, as at New York, we boys were very eager to see what was to be seen. We roamed the place in all directions, admiring the handsome houses with their fine marble steps, the plated knockers on the doors, and the broad brick pavement duly washed every morning, and coloured with red ochre. We often visited the market, which, for size and abundance of good things, I believe is nowhere equalled in the world.

Having engaged cheap lodgings about seventeen miles distant, at a place called Village Green, we left Philadelphia, and about mid-day we reached our destination. The house was a frame one, and stood almost alone, "a little above the stars," as Joel Swayne, our landlord, expressed it ; that is to say a little further up the road than the inn called the "Seven Stars." Altogether the place looked rather forlorn ; but we were quite disposed to make ourselves contented ; and we entered at once upon American rural life.

Joel Swayne was a small farmer. He kept a horse

and cow; and it became my province to milk the cow. Having,, however, an abundance of leisure on our hands, we employed much of our time in roaming about the neighbouring woods and fields.

The weather had set in excessively hot, and we boys soon adopted the practice of the country people and left off our shoes and stockings. This. practice is one of the greatest luxuries of a warm climate. Our feet were tender at first, and we often made them bleed ; yet they soon hardened, and. by sliding them along we were even able to walk over a clover field after it had been mown. If, in our rambles, we came to a run of water, how refreshing it was to dabble about in it till our feet were cooled, and then pursue our way !

Christopher was the proud possessor of a gun ; and he took an early opportunity of showing us his proficiency in the art of using it.

In our fishing operations, our success was unsatisfactory. There was a mill-dam about half a mile off which we used sometimes to visit. It was almost encircled by woods, and was a lonely, sultry, dreamy nook, where I have sometimes felt a sensation of awe, mingled with fear, such as I never felt in any other place. I believe it was partly occasioned by the number of water-snakes which frequented the place, of which we all had a great horror. We were afraid to bathe because of them.

Having prepared two eel-lines, we laid them over-night in the head water. Early in the morning we hastened to see what we had caught. We began to pull up our lines slowly, and were surprised to find

D

that the ends of them were carried out of the water
and brought to the bank and buried in the mud.
However we pulled away at them, and, to our
astonishment, found that we had caught two large
terrapins, or water-turtles, commonly called snap-
ping turtles, from the unyielding tenacity with which
they bite.

Another adventure of ours I must not omit. One
fine day we took a walk in search of fox-grapes, to make
a pie with. These grapes are a kind that grow wild.
They are remarkably large and tempting to the eye ;
but very sour and nauseous. Their name, therefore,
is doubly significant. Well, having searched a long
time, we at length came to a field, at the farther
end of which we espied a bush overrun with a wild
vine. We hastened to it ; and, on peeping through
the leaves to discover if there were any grapes, we
were horrified to perceive a large black snake close
to us, suspended amongst the branches. We started
back a few steps in the greatest alarm, and ignorant
what to do. We had heard a great many frightful
stories about snakes, and we had a strong antipathy
to them. Christopher had his gun with him as usual,
and he resolved to fire ; but not being able to see the
snake where he stood, and, therefore, being uncertain
whether he had shot it, he was not satisfied without
giving it another volley. So he loaded his gun
again, and once more fired away at the bush.

We saw nothing of the snake ; and all was still.
After waiting awhile we summoned up resolution
enough to approach the bush and peep through the
leaves. To our great satisfaction there hung the

snake quite dead. We were afraid, however, to pull it out; but made the best of our way home, and related our exploit.

By the next day our courage had revived enough to enable us to go again to the place. We found the snake in the same situation in which we left it; and, drawing it forth, carried it home in triumph. It measured nearly five feet in length.

These black snakes are sometimes called racers; and I have myself seen them glide downhill with astonishing rapidity.

In the meantime my father was busily occupied in visiting a number of farms that were to be disposed of in different directions. But he saw nothing that quite pleased him. One objection to almost all of them was, that the springs were always dried up in hot weather.

At length, therefore, he set off for Susquehanna county, a newly-settled district. After an absence of about three weeks he returned well satisfied that it would never do to take his family there.

It would take up too much of my space to relate my father's various adventures during this journey. His ride along the " Narrows," with mountains towering above his head on one side, and the River Susquehanna sixty feet beneath him on the other; how he dined at a house, and, falling into a pleasant chat with the landlord, went away and forgot to pay for his dinner; how he travelled through a burnt forest twenty miles in extent; how he lost his way in the woods; his adventure with an old woman, who accommodated him with her little black tobacco-

pipe in his utmost need ; how he was beset by land
speculators ; how he saw a log-house built in one
afternoon; his meeting with a party of half-savage
hunters in the woods; all these, and many other
matters, served, for years afterwards, to afford topics
for agreeable narrations over his evening pipe.

Although we were disposed to make ourselves
happy at Village Green, yet we underwent many
privations there.

We were badly off both for good bread, and also a
supply of fresh meat. We obtained the latter once
a week; but, owing to the intense heat, it would not
keep. Not the least of our privations was the want
of good water. Our own pump and the pumps in
the neighbourhood became dry ; we had, therefore,
to fetch it from a considerable distance.

The summer was now wearing away, when my
father heard of a farm for sale on the Delaware.
As he considered that the more he saw of the
country before he settled the better, and as the
farm lay in a district that he had not yet visited, he
resolved to go and see it. However, he was again
disappointed, for, though the farm pleased him well,
the owner had altered his mind about parting with it.

The day was intensely warm ; and, after walking
over the farm, through fields of Indian corn that
reached three feet above his head, where scarcely a
breath of air was stirring, he set off to walk to
Wilmington, on his way home.

At this town resided a certain Dr. Gibbons, a
member of the Society of Friends, whom he had met
with once, and who had invited him to his house

if he ever came that way. Weary as he was, the country through which he was travelling pleased him much better than any that he had before seen in America, and when the handsome town of Wilmington burst upon his sight, he was taken with pleasurable surprise. On the whole, my father was so well satisfied with the town and his new acquaintance that he resolved to take my mother there. They were received with great kindness by their new friends, and arrangements were soon made for the removal of the family to this town.

CHAPTER IV.

Residence at Wilmington—Typhus fever—Death of Lucy—
  " Lucy's Grave "—Illness and recovery of others—Kindness of sympathising friends — Anecdotes of Quaker
  ministers.

THE woods had begun to put on their autumnal
appearance when, without regret, we bade farewell
for ever to Village Green.   We had hired a tilted
waggon for the occasion, which held our boxes and
ourselves on the top of them.   In this style we proceeded on our journey; and, after a rough ride, in
which we could see but little of the country through
the holes in the tilt, we reached Wilmington in the
afternoon.   The town, at this period, contained about
six thousand inhabitants; and, standing on a gentle
hill, presented a beautiful appearance.   In front, in
full view, at the distance of about two miles, the
broad river Delaware rolled its vast waters.   On
each side of the town flowed a smaller river, which,
winding through the meadows below, at length
united, and, after taking another graceful sweep, fell
into the Delaware.   The principal thoroughfare of
the town, about a mile in length, extended over the
brow of the hill from one of these smaller rivers to
the other, each of which was crossed by a bridge.
As the spectator stands with his face towards the
Delaware, the one of these rivers which is on the
right is the Christiana, an ample stream capable of

bearing ships upon its surface, but turbid, dull, and uninteresting, flowing through flat and marshy fields. The one on his left is the Brandywine, a river much smaller in volume, but incomparably more beautiful, rippling through a wild region, and adorned with rocky precipitous banks, covered with calmias, wild-vines, and graceful forest trees.

Our house stood in the principal street, on the highest part of the hill. It was, however, old and dilapidated, and had been empty some time. From the back of it we caught a view of the Delaware, which made it more pleasant from the number of vessels that were constantly passing.

Our friends at Wilmington were very kind in welcoming us to our new abode. Before we had purchased any chairs we had a company of friends to tea. Boxes were arranged round the room for seats, while a larger one answered the purpose of a table, and very happy we made ourselves. It can hardly be denied that there must have been some-thing about the members of our family that attracted favour. My father's and mother's entertaining and unassuming qualities pleased the Americans, and, accustomed as they were to emigrants from the north of England, it was a frequent compliment which they paid to us, that we talked as good English as themselves. Above all, my sister Lucy attracted admiration. Her fine features, her sim-plicity of manners, and her good sense, improved by education, made her a general favourite. On oui part we were equally well pleased with our new friends and with the town. We could now supply ourselves with every commodity that we wanted; and, as there were two markets in the week, provisions were to be obtained in great abundance, and extremely cheap. Having provided ourselves with a little furniture, and having received our large store packages from the warehouse in Philadelphia, and added to our comfort by their contents, we now felt ourselves settled for the approaching winter.

The cold weather had already set in when my sister Lucy, whose health had for some time been delicate, was taken unwell. A kind friend of ours, Lydia Aldrich, happening to call, and finding that Lucy's disorder did not yield to the usual treatment, felt her pulse, and at once recommended us to send for Dr. Gibbons. Being in a land of strangers, and our house very incompletely furnished, we were ill-prepared for sickness; but so it was. Our friend the physician soon came. On the following morning, she was evidently worse. In the course of the day, perceiving herself that she was no better, she said to her father, very emphatically, "Father, dost thou think that I shall die?" He replied, "My dear child, I think thou wilt not; I trust thou wilt be spared to us awhile longer." She rejoined, "But dost thou know I shall not die?" He replied, "No, I do not know: but if, my dear, it should please the Almighty to remove thee from us, tell me, dost thou feel peace of mind?" She reflected awhile, and then, in her diffident manner replied, "On looking over my past life, I do not remember that I have ever done anything much amiss; but, father, is it wicked to have bad thoughts?" He told her, "No, excepting so far as they were given way to, then they became sinful, but not otherwise." My father and mother kneeling by her bedside, and weeping over her, she proceeded, " I have prayed against them—from my infantile days I have prayed against them ; but I am sensible I have not been so watchful as I ought to have been, particularly in meetings. I am almost too weak to pray ; do you pray for me." After awhile she added, " I know the Almighty is no respecter of persons, and that though our sins may have been as scarlet, He can make them white as snow." Then, throwing her arms out of bed, and clasping her hands in an attitude of supplication, she exclaimed, " Oh, Lord God, look down on me, a poor creature ! I think I should like to live awhile longer, if it be Thy will, on my dear mother's account ; on no other account would I desire it. I think I am quite willing to leave the world, if I might be permitted to enter one of those mansions whose walls are salvation, and whose gates are praise ; where the weary are at rest, and where the wicked cease from troubling. Praise, honour, and glory, be ascribed unto Thee, who art worthy, for evermore. Amen ! "

It soon appeared that her complaint was no other than that dreadful one, the typhus fever. The dark cloud of domestic affliction had indeed fallen upon us !

As soon as our friends knew that sickness had broken out in our family, their warmest sympathies were called forth on our account, and they displayed the uncommon kindness of their dispositions. Some, we knew not who, sent us bedding and other furniture.

Some kind friends sat up with our invalids, for by this time my mother was laid up with an attack of pleurisy; while two others, whose names I shall always hold in veneration, Lydia Aldrich and Margaret Morton, came on alternate days to attend upon my mother and sister. Our friend, Margaret Morton, very nearly fell a victim to her generous kindness to us; she caught the typhus fever, and was brought so low that her recovery was almost despaired of; but she revived, and lived to favour us ever afterwards with her friendship.

Often, when I look back on this period of my life, and remember the kindness of these friends to us in our deep affliction in a strange land, far away from our relations and our former friends, my eyes overflow with irrepressible tears.

My sister Lucy soon became aware of the improbability of her recovery. After a few days a stupor came on. On the 8th of First Month the physician perceived symptoms of approaching dissolution. One or two of our friends were kindly with us to witness the last sad scene. The little mournful company around my sister's bed maintained now a solemn silence, awaiting her last breath. That breath she soon breathed. There was no struggle, not even the discomposure of her beautiful and placid countenance, and her joyous spirit was translated to the world of rest.

But the season of affliction was not yet over. My dear mother, distressed beyond expression at the death of her eldest child — her companion — grew increasingly ill. In a few days my brother sickened, and it soon became obvious that he, too, was attacked with typhus fever. He became rapidly worse, and grew delirious. Meanwhile my father, worn with grief, fatigue, and anxiety, exerted himself to the utmost in watching and waiting upon them, allowing himself no rest neither by day nor night, till his strength became so exhausted that if he sat down in a chair he instantly fell asleep. At this time the weather was so intensely cold that, although blankets were nailed before the windows and a large fire was kept blazing, yet water. froze in the sick room. It was now my turn to be taken down with the fever, and soon afterwards our Christopher. Our attacks, however, were of a milder character. But I will not prolong my painful narrative with further particulars. Having had about three months of severe domestic affliction, it was now that we were getting better that our kind neighbours displayed once more their sympathy and benevolence. They inundated us with presents of good things. Whatever was adapted to recruit the strength of invalids was not forgotten.

Who is there that remembers his once happy fireside circle being first broken—that remembers the first inroad of death into his beloved family—but feels a response in his bosom at this recital of our affliction !

There is something in the first death in a happy domestic group which casts around a peculiar melancholy. No one can tell what death is till its victim is the beloved being at one's side. Every pleasant recollection is then embittered by association with

the memory of that beloved one who was and is not.
Every theme of family conversation leads to one
mournful subject, and every thought is tinged with
one pervading sorrow.　Such was our case when we
once more collected around our social hearth, and saw
and felt that one of us was missing.　In our sadness
we naturally looked back to our own country.　We
suffered the more because we were in a foreign clime,
far away from our relations, and we felt an inexpres-
sible yearning for our native land.

Here may be aptly introduced a poem written by
him some years later :—

LUCY'S GRAVE.

Far away o'er the turbulent wave,
　Far away from this soft azure sky,
The breezes, around the sad grave
　Of my Lucy, at evening sigh ;
Full oft to that grave, when on high
　The pale moon shines pensively clear,
On the light wings of fancy I fly,
　And shed o'er my Lucy a tear.

The same moon looks down on the place
　Of her peaceful, but dreamless, repose ;
And the sun, at the end of his race,
　His parting beam over it throws ;
The tall summer grass on it grows,
　Gently waving when light winds arise,
And the night-hawk, at evening's close,
　Hovers round it and plaintively cries.

And there, o'er my loved Lucy's grave,
  In battle the thunder-clouds meet;
And round it the wintry winds rave,
  And the merciless hurricanes beat.
Yet thy slumber, my Lucy, is sweet
  As the spring flowers that over thee bloom,
And as silent and soft thy retreat,
  As the light snow that falls on thy tomb.

Yes, my Lucy, far off is thy grave
  From the scenes of thine infantile glee;
But though thou art o'er the wide wave,
  Thou art ofttimes remembered by me.
For cold must my young bosom be,
  And the powers of my memory slight,
If my love could e'er lessen for thee,
  Or thy worth could grow dim in my sight.

But thy spirit is flown to the skies,
  To those mansions from misery free,
Which are not for the brave, or the wise,
  But the pure and the humble like thee.
And the thought is consoling to me—
  Thou art gone to that happier sphere;
For this life is a billowy sea,
  And every billow a tear.

Fare thee well, then, my Lucy, farewell!
  Long shall peace linger round thy last home,
While the night-hawk above seems to tell
  Of her woe at thy premature doom.
The spring flowers shall over thee bloom;
  The breezes at evening shall sigh;
And the moonbeams flow down to thy tomb,
  From their beautiful fount in the sky.

And the Brandywine, too, shall still flow
    Down its rocks and green vales as of yore;
And at night, when the winds cease to blow,
    Thy requiem shall be its deep roar.
Fare thee well, my loved Lucy! Once more
    A long and a fervent farewell!—
May we meet, when my journey is o'er,
    In the land where the purified dwell.

Several reasons rendered it desirable for us to remove from the house which we now occupied. We therefore hired a neat red-bricked house at the corner of Wood and Tatnall Streets. To this house we removed on the 25th of Third Month. A friend observed to my father that there was now an excellent opening for a school, as the master of a day-school which was kept in a room belonging to the Society was going to leave. He applied for the mastership, and was duly chosen. We opened the school with four or five scholars, and, in the course of a few months, we had thirty boys.

About this time my mind appeared to receive a new impulse. I became exceedingly fond of reading. My mother recommended me to read Falconer's " Shipwreck." I began it; and from that time I may date my love of poetry.

Our Christopher had, all along, displayed ingenious talents and uncommon ability in the art of bargain-making. He was the leading spirit in our boyish speculations. It is the custom of the American housewives to make their own soft soap. It is simply ley, from their wood ashes, boiled with kitchen grease. The product is a beautiful jelly. To make it *come* is a matter of skill, and many fail in it. My mother tried and failed. Christopher asked permission to try; and was eminently successful. In consequence he conceived the plan of making it for sale. My brother and I entered into his scheme; and we soon opened a little trade. We bought a couple of old oil hogsheads and made ley tubs of them; and proceeded in our enterprise with boyish spirit. Though our trade was small our profits were good.

An acquaintance, who was a shoemaker in the town, kindly offered to instruct us boys in the art of shoemaking, on condition that we never would set up against him. As it seemed desirable to be acquainted with a handicraft trade, we availed ourselves of his offer; and set to work resolutely with our awls and wax-ends, and learned soon to make shoes. As to myself, after practising the various branches of the art, I made one pair of shoes wholly with my own hands, which were sufficiently decent for me to wear. Having completed my task I relinquished for the future all connection with leather and lapstone.

It was, I believe, during the winter of 1821 that my brother and I attended a number of familiar lectures on "electricity" and the "laws of matter." They were delivered by Dr. Gibbons to his sons; and he kindly invited us to hear them. In order to imprint them on our memory he repeated each lecture several times. This plan was a good one; and, being thus well grounded in the subjects, we derived much advantage from our attendance. We acquired, in this way, something of a taste for natural philosophy; and the acquisition of every new taste is a new source of enjoyment.

As the school brought us in a maintenance we launched out in our expenditure so far as to hire a mulatto girl as a servant. As we now lived in the town we were more in the way of having casual visitors. The Americans are a social people, and use but little ceremony in their intercourse with each other. It was no uncommon thing for us to have several of our friends call upon us unexpectedly of an evening to indulge in pleasant conversation, and smoke cigars with my father.

I must not omit to describe one of our friends who frequently spent an evening with us. His name was Benjamin Ferris, a surveyor by profession. His countenance beamed with intelligence and cheerfulness; and his voice was musically sweet. In conversation he excelled all others that I have ever heard. His very smile was electrical. There was refinement in whatever he said; yet there was nothing of effort or affectation about him. In his fascinating company hours passed away without being noticed. While listening to him one might at once give credence to those reported powers of conversation which are associated with the names of Coleridge, Burns, and Savage. The society of such a man could not fail to give a bias to my opening mind. His sister Deborah, who was married to Joseph Bringhurst, a chemist, and a friend of the celebrated Robert Fulton, was the most extraordinary woman with whom I was ever acquainted. It was not her person, however, but her mind and

manners, and powers of conversation, which distinguished her. She became my mother's most intimate
and valued friend.

Another of our visitors was William Poole, one of
the great Brandywine millers. He was a man of
extensive information, affable, and full of anecdote.
As a specimen I shall insert one which he told us
respecting Thomas Colley, who was, originally, a
drummer in the English Militia, and afterwards
became a minister in the Society of Friends, and
paid a visit to America in that capacity. While
travelling in that country he came to Richmond, in
Virginia, at which town he felt a religious concern to
hold a public meeting. There was no building in
the place so suitable for his purpose as the Hall of
Legislature, which was then sitting. As soon as it
became known to them that an English Quaker
preacher was desirous to have the hall to hold a
meeting in they adjourned their sitting and allowed
him to have the use of it. Several members of the
Legislature attended, and, among the rest, the gentleman who related the following particulars. He
said that when he sat down in the meeting he felt
ashamed of himself for being there; and he was still
more ashamed when the preacher rose, and he perceived that he was a little, insignificant man, and,
evidently, uneducated. He thought it presumptuous
in Thomas Colley to pretend to come there to
enlighten them, who were men of education. He
hung down his head in order that he might not be
observed by any one present. He said that the text
of Scripture with which the preacher began was one

E

that he had never been able to understand, and,
therefore, had disbelieved, It was this, "Except a
man be born again he cannot see the kingdom of
God." He was rather struck to hear Thomas
Colley pronounce this text; and wondered what he
would make of it. At first the preacher spoke with
extreme slowness; but as he proceeded with his
subject, and explained the text according to its
spiritual meaning, he waxed warmer and warmer,
till the gentleman began to be deeply interested in the
discourse. At length he ventured to look up at the
preacher; and he said that he could not help fancy-
ing that it was an angel to whom he was listening
and not a man. Somehow or other his tears, he
said, began to flow; and on stealing a glance around
he observed that many of those about him were
affected in the same manner. It was an occasion
such as he had never witnessed before; and, at the
conclusion of the discourse, he felt that he had been
enlightened and edified. As soon as the meeting
was over several of the legislative body who had
been present collected to discuss the merits of the
sermon. They had all been very much gratified
with it; and it was proposed, and immediately
resolved upon, to make up a purse of money, and
depute one or two of their number to present it to
Thomas Colley, with a request that he would allow
his sermon to be printed. The deputation accordingly
proceeded to his tavern, where they were introduced to
the friend who travelled with him as his companion.
Having stated their business to him they were surprised to be informed that the discourse, with which

they had been so much pleased, was preached without premeditation, and that it was in vain to offer money to Thomas Colley, as the ministers in the Society of Friends never received any pay for their sermons, except the " penny of peace."

Another of our frequent visitors was Evan Lewis, a tanner by business, who was rather a prominent character in the Society. He possessed an enlightened mind and extensive information; and was a warm philanthropist, and an especial friend to the negro race. Evan Lewis, being a man of a social disposition and fond of anecdote, we often had his company. It is for the sake of another story respecting an English Quaker preacher that I mention him. The incident to which I refer is the account of a visit paid by William Crotch to Cowper, the poet. William Crotch was a man in very humble life, and could scarcely read or write, but was a deeply religious character, and possessed in an extraordinary degree the gift of spiritual discernment. Being once in the neighbourhood of Cowper he felt a religious concern to pay him a visit. He accordingly went to the house. A man-servant came to the door. William Crotch requested to be introduced to his master, but the servant replied that his master saw no one, and he had strict injunctions not to admit anybody. William Crotch was rather disconcerted at this refusal, and he continued to urge his request; but still in vain. At length he said, " Go and tell thy master that a poor creature like himself wishes to see him." The servant carried the message in, and presently returned with his master's permission to

introduce the stranger.   On entering the room where
the poet was sitting, William Crotch walked up to
him, and, without any other salutation, took him by
the hand, and sat down by his side.   For one whole
hour they thus sat hand in hand, without speaking a
word.   In relating the circumstance, William Crotch
said that during the time that they thus sat in solemn
silence a clear conviction was afforded him of the
extraordinary purity of Cowper's mind.   He at
length addressed the poet, and, having in this way
disburdened his spirit, he took leave of him, well
satisfied that he had obtained the interview.

William Crotch went to America, and in the course
of his travels paid a religious visit to the family in
which our friend Evan Lewis was a boarder when
he was a young man.   Evan Lewis, at that time,
was rather a wild youth, and he had no inclination to
be present at the sitting, and he therefore absented
himself.   William Crotch inquired whether all the
family were present.   He was answered in the
affirmative.   He, however, seemed rather dissatis-
fied, and made some further inquiry.   He was then
informed that there was a young man who was a
boarder in the family who was not present.   William
Crotch desired to have his company, and on being
sent for Evan Lewis rather unwillingly complied.
Knowing something of the character of William
Crotch, he trembled with apprehension ; and his
worst fears were soon realised, for the preacher
directed nearly the whole of his discourse to him.
When the sitting was over, William Crotch, as is
usual on such occasions, shook hands with all the

company. Evan Lewis was glad that the time of his deliverance was come. He was disappointed, however, for William Crotch, on shaking hands with him, said, " Young man, I have not done with thee yet ! "

They accordingly had a private sitting, in the course of which William Crotch addressed him in the most extraordinary manner, as if he had known him all his life, and had been the depository of all his secrets. Evan Lewis assured us that William Crotch mentioned circumstances to him which he had thought nobody in the world knew of but himself. The occasion was one never to be forgotten.

I have several times heard my father relate the following anecdote. George Dillwyn, of Burlington, New Jersey, U.S., was an eminent minister of the Society of Friends at the beginning of this century. He was very remarkable for his spiritual discernment into the religious states of individuals, and other mysterious mental impressions. On one occasion, when sitting in the parlour with his wife, he suddenly rose from his seat, took his hat, and seemed about to go out for a walk. His wife attempted to detain him. She told him that it rained (of which he seemed to be unaware), and also said that it was nearly dinner time. He replied that he *must* go. He could not explain this feeling of necessity, but only obeyed the impulse which he felt. His wife, therefore, fetched him an umbrella, and away he set off along the street, without knowing what was his destination. By and by he came opposite a house, and felt prompted to open the door and walk in—an act quite in accordance with the free and unceremonious habits of the country. On entering the front parlour he found two men, who appeared greatly astonished to see him. He sat down by them in silence, and then said that he had felt impelled to enter that house, though for what purpose he could not tell; but perhaps they could inform him. They then told him that they had been having an earnest discussion on the doctrine of a particular Providence. One of them stoutly maintained this doctrine, while the other as strenuously argued against it. The dispute ran high between them. At length the latter said that if Mr. Dillwyn were to walk into the room at that instant he would believe the doctrine. He had no sooner said the words than, said he, "you came in." After this remarkable incident George Dillwyn addressed them in an impressive manner, and then took his leave.

Our present house being small, we boys had no room to carry on our little manufactory of soft soap. We therefore obtained the use of an old oil-house close by. Having bought an iron boiler, we undertook to fix it up in this place, and set to work with the industry of so many ants. We got some brickbats, and made some mortar, and without, as far as I know, ever having seen a boiler hung, commenced operations. Having hung our boiler, we had the satisfaction to find that the furnace drew remarkably well. We now commenced soap making on a rather larger scale, and we made money fast. As we had been taught from early life not to spend it in cakes and oranges, we became substantial little men. My father was our banker, and in order to encourage us he gave us good interest. Our soap-making business, though small, was so profitable that the thought occurred to my father to set up as a soap manufacturer. Although the school brought him in a living, yet he disliked the occupation, and wished to introduce his sons into some advantageous business. He was a man who devoutly desired that all his steps should be rightly directed. After much consideration, therefore, in the present, concern, he concluded to proceed in it.

It was now autumn. My father in the meantime had been to Philadelphia and bought ash tubs, iron pans, and other apparatus, at a very low price. I now finished my school-boy days, and with Christopher was employed in many duties connected with the business. My brother was too useful to my father in the school to be often with us. The way in which we commenced was to do a little business and do it well. We made our commodities of excellent materials, and sold our goods at reasonable prices, and thus we procured customers. Our profits, nevertheless, were large, and we soon began to prosper.

About this time we took into our family a little foster child of about three years of age. Her name was Grace Mitchell. Her mother had died and left a family of eight small children, and, according to the custom of the country, her friends took them into their families to bring up, or else procured situations for them elsewhere. In this instance the family of the child were entire strangers to us.

At first little Grace preserved a complete silence.

For a few days she hardly lifted her eyes from the
ground, and uttered not a word. She often sighed
deeply, and there seemed to be something that
weighed heavily on her little heart.   But after a time
she brightened up and became a very pleasant addition to our family. Poor dear little orphan ! what
were thy feelings when thou didst find thyself among
strangers ? Was it the thought of thy dead mother
that saddened thee ? Thou wast a beautiful and an
amiable child ; and, when the sense of thy early loss
and infantine affliction had passed away, how did thy
young heart bound again with spontaneous happiness.
If thou art still alive, a blessing on thy head !

The neighbourhood of Wilmington afforded great
facilities for fishing, bathing, and skating, as well as
shooting ; and we boys were not so bound down as
not to avail ourselves of them occasionally. Of
bathing and skating I was excessively fond ; while
the marshes below the town, along the banks of the
Delaware, which were frequented by immense flocks
of blackbirds and reed birds, were an irresistible
temptation to Christopher.

These shooting excursions remind me of a lively
little Frenchman of the name of Joseph Zambier,
who dwelt within a stone's throw of our house, who
was very fond of shooting. He was a blacksmith by
business, but had travelled far and seen much of the
mutations of human life. Originally he was a soldier
in the army of Napoleon, and had fought on the
burning plains of Egypt. He subsequently took up
his abode in St. Domingo. While he was residing
there with his wife the memorable and bloody Revo-

lution in that island occurred. At that dreadful time
of anarchy and massacre the whites were in the
utmost danger. In the confusion of the times poor
Joseph Zambier and his wife, while attempting to
make their escape, were separated, and each supposed
that the other was killed. His wife, however, managed
to get on board a vessel and reached Philadelphia,
where she went into service. She remained in that
city a year or two, as well as I remember. One
day, as she was sweeping the pavement before the
door of the house where she lived, a gentleman came
along, who, perceiving perhaps by the handkerchief
tied jauntily round her head that she was a foreigner,
stopped and inquired of her if she knew where a man
of the name of Joseph Zambier lived. She threw
down her broom in astonishment, and exclaimed,
" Can you tell *me* where he lives ? " The gentleman
replied that he worked somewhere in that neighbourhood, but he was not certain where. It was true.
He had escaped in another vessel and had reached
Philadelphia, where he had obtained employment as
a blacksmith. The poor woman, overjoyed at the
intelligence that he was alive, would not leave the
gentleman, but quitted her work and accompanied
him in search of her husband. With a little further
inquiry they found the shop where he worked. On
entering it, there was poor Joseph Zambier ! The
hammer dropped from his hand at the sight of his
wife, and they flew into each other's arms.

CHAPTER V.

Return voyage to England —Violent storm—A ship on fire—
Safe arrival.

It was in the autumn of the present year, 1824, that a circumstance occurred which formed the commencement of a new era in my life.

I was at work one day in the factory when my father came over to say that I was wanted at home as soon as I was at liberty.

I soon went over; when my father had collected us all in the parlour, he informed us of the death of his Aunt Rebecca Barritt, and of a handsome legacy which she had kindly left us. It was quite a scene. We were almost bewildered with joyful amazement. The absorbing thought which took possession of us was, that we might now return to our own country. It was true that we had an increasing business and a fair prospect before us; but we loved our own country best; we were able to return to it, and we soon made our resolve. When our friends were informed of our intended return there was a general feeling of regret expressed.

We found but little difficulty in disposing of our business; and once more the time came round to undertake the mighty task of packing up for a sea voyage.

Our little foster-child, Grace Mitchell, had now to go to a new home. We were sorry to part with the dear little creature, and her friends would willingly have allowed us to take her with us ; but it appeared undesirable.

Having packed up everything that we intended to take with us, then came the sale of the rest of our furniture and effects. It proved a good one.

Being now without a home, our friends kindly took us in for a day or two, which we occupied in paying farewell visits. This was a sorrowful task. We had been treated with great kindness by many of them in times of affliction and distress, and the parting with them was very painful.

The morning at length arrived for our departure for Philadelphia in order to embark.

We took breakfast at the house of our friend Joseph Bringhurst. A number of our other friends met us here to accompany us to the steamboat, which soon parted from her moorings, and ploughed her way between the winding banks of the Christiana into the broad waters of the Delaware. Wilmington was long in sight ; and as we gazed upon it from a distance, how many thoughts rushed upon our minds. It was there that we had known such various vicissitudes and adventures ; there our hearts had sunk so low, and there our hearts had bounded so high and joyously ; there, too, were so many that we loved and valued, and there was Lucy's grave !

On arriving at Philadelphia we paid a visit to the ship *Electra*, in which we were going to sail. We found the steerage was a small and wretched hole ; and as our circumstances were now improved, we agreed to take our passage in the cabin at the rate of

100 dols. for each. For several days we were occupied in preparing for our voyage, paying and receiving visits, and going to see whatever was remarkable in the city. Among other places we visited the spot where grew the venerable elm-tree under which William Penn made his Christian treaty with the aborigines of the country. The day of our embarkation was the 8th of the Fourth Month, 1824.

Some incidents of the home voyage may here be quoted from the journal of his sister Ann :—

" On the 22nd we experienced one of the most sudden transitions in the weather that anyone on board had ever witnessed. From the enjoyment of a beautifully serene morning we were called upon to experience one of the most awful storms. We were seated at dinner, and Absalom, the mulatto cabinboy, who had been sent on deck to call our first mate, came in haste with the intelligence that a yard-arm was just snapped in two by the wind. This was so very unexpected that Captain Robinson instantly ran on deck to ascertain the extent of the damage. It very soon began to rain, and continued almost without intermission until about six o'clock, when it ceased and we expected a return of fine weather. We were seated at the tea-table waiting for Captain Robinson, who was changing his wet clothes. As he was doing so he perceived a sudden alteration in the wind by the motion of the ship; and so imminent was the danger that he was obliged instantly to go on deck without coat, hat, or shoes, and remained without the latter for two hours. We were alarmed at the extraordinary motion of the vessel. The wind howled with the utmost violence, the sea raged, and the rain poured down in torrents. I never before felt anything so awful. It seemed as if old Ocean were determined to convince us of his own power and our impotence. We were buried in the deep and then lifted up on the pinnacle of a mountain wave, where the vessel hung for a moment and trembled like a leaf or a feather, and then again plunged headlong into the fathomless abyss. The loud roaring of the contending elements must be heard to convey a correct idea.

"About ten o'clock Captain Robinson came down for a few minutes. We congratulated him on his safety. He said he believed we were now out of danger. It was a most providential circumstance that we had but two sails up at the time; if we had had one more he says he has no doubt but that the vessel would have been lost. Captain Robinson has crossed the ocean fifty-four times, and he says he never witnessed anything like this for suddenness and violence.

"On the 24th a small cloud of smoke was dis- covered to the north-west of us. We were now in lat. 42° 20'; long. 39° 15'. Our second mate instantly ran up the rigging and confirmed our suspicions by the appalling cry of 'Fire!'

"The sound ran through the ship like an electric shock, many supposing it to be our own vessel on fire. It was about six p.m., the sky dark and lowering; we neared it rapidly and soon could plainly distinguish that it was indeed a large ship on fire.

Oh, what was all that we had seen, all that we had heard, compared with what we now saw! It is impossible to give an adequate description of our feelings. Men were now sent aloft to look out for boats, as it was beyond a doubt that the poor unhappy sufferers were either already consumed, or had taken to their boats, as the masts of the vessel were burnt down. We could distinguish its hull and distinctly smell the smoke.

" The vessel being now directly to windward of us, the captain said it would be three hours before we could approach nearer to it, as we must go considerably beyond it, and so get on the other side. It now began to grow dark, but we all thought, improbable as it was that we could save the sufferers, we ought to do all that lay in our power, and we accordingly hung out a large light and bore away on the other tack. We were, as near as we could judge, about a mile from the fire at dark. All hope of rendering the crew any assistance was now at an end, and we contemplated this sublime but awful spectacle with feelings indescribable. To be so near the unfortunate sufferers and yet feel it impossible to snatch them from such a dreadful death was indeed distressing, and caused a deep and saddening gloom to prevail amongst us all. We lay by a considerable length of time, but it appearing to Captain Robinson useless to wait any longer, he reluctantly gave orders to spread the sails and pursue our voyage, at the same time declaring that he had used his utmost endeavours to save the lives of the crew. We left the poor creatures to their fate, sincerely hoping they had been picked up by some other vessel.

" After our arrival we learned that the vessel we had seen on fire was the *Hannibal*, from Virginia. It was struck by lightning. Five persons perished. The remainder, finding it impossible to save the vessel, escaped in their boat, and were picked up by a brig and carried to England.

" 27th.—Although it is such a sweet evening our barometers, the noisy geese, prognosticate stormy weather. We place great confidence in them as they were very correct in the case of the memorable 22nd.

" 5th of May.—About ten a.m. we were gratified with the intelligence that land was discovered from the mast head—the Scilly Isles—at about nine leagues distance.

" 6th.—To-day we were greeted with the joyful sight of old England, which appears like a little streak of fine mist along the horizon. A great number of vessels of all descriptions are sailing in all directions. Although the evening is cloudy it is one of the most beautiful sunsets I ever saw ; a large crimson cloud, towering to a vast height, reflects a bright glow over the whole surface of the water, and we appear as if floating on a sea of gold.

" 10th.—At twelve o'clock we arrived at the London Docks ; but while the vessel was in the act of being towed round the corner the rope broke, and before it could be replaced the tide became too low to proceed, and we were obliged to cast anchor in the middle of the river.

" 11*th.*—Having all our parcels previously arranged, we had nothing to do but to inform the officer, who happened to be a very civil man, that we wished to go ashore. He then came down and, slightly glancing over them, told us we were at liberty. Our boatman, fortunately for our escape from the officers on the wharf, who no doubt would have ransacked our parcels, rowed us as far as the Tower stairs, where, to our great joy, we landed without interruption."

Thus after an absence of five years, all but a few days, did we found ourselves once more in Old England. Having no place of permanent settlement in view, we removed from our London lodgings to Henley; and as we had no further need of the services of Christopher, my father gave him up his indentures, and he went home to his native village.

CHAPTER VI.

Return to Kelvedon—Friendship with the Bowman family—
Various early Poems : "When Friend meets Friend"—
"My First Grey Hair"—"From Grave to Gay"—
"Hope"—"Death of Martha"—Death of his younger
sister—"My Sisters."

IN order to make a little change my father took
a journey to Norwich with William and myself.
We visited the Mile-end house, in which Aunt Barritt
had lived, and also Hellesden Hall, beyond Norwich,
in which her ancestors had dwelt. On our return
through Essex we visited Boreham and Kelvedon,
the scenes of my childhood. Every object appeared
to be diminished about one-half in size, and though
it was very pleasant to see once more old faces and
places, yet there seemed a pervading dulness every-
where.

I must here mention an incident which happened
to myself, as it had, I believe, a permanent influence
upon me; and it is, therefore, right that I should
record it. I was walking one day in a lane near
Henley, in a somewhat melancholy mood, when my
heart was suddenly warmed with a divine influence.
It seemed as if a holy glow pervaded my inmost soul.
It was, I believe, a manifestation of the love of God
to me. I felt His kindling presence, and, as I stood

F

and leaned against a gate, tears of mingled joy and sorrow flowed from my eyes.

I believe that all are blessed with similar divine visitations; and it is well if they are looked back upon as promptings to virtuous conduct in the time of temptation, and as sources of true consolation in the days of adversity.

After awhile we removed to Kelvedon, to which place we seemed more attached than to any other. Having but little to engage my time and attention I, at this time, by way of occupation, made a vigorous incursion among our books. Among other works I read the " Spectator," and also Beattie's " Minstrel," which had once been a task to me, but was now a delightful employment, for my mind had begun to expand.

My principal favourites, however, were Johnson's " Lives of the Poets," and Blair's " Lectures on Rhetoric," &c. These I studied with profound interest. The " Lives of the Poets " inflamed my ambition, while Blair's " Lectures " seemed to embody principles and illustrations which already existed in my mind. They seemed, as it were, to call into life and activity my latent knowledge, and render palpable what before was unperceived. In the spring we resolved to make another move. The dear old corner house, which we left when we went to America, was vacant. We accordingly hired it, and thus, after all our wanderings and adventures, we returned to the very spot from which we had set out.

There was at this time living at Kelvedon an ancient lady of the name of Elizabeth Day. She

was a sprightly old-fashioned dame, with never a
gray hair in her head. This cheerful old lady had
a family of grand-daughters of the name of Bowman,
some of whom always lived with her. With this
family especially we young folks formed a close
intimacy. Their youngest brother Alfred had been
my schoolfellow at Colne, and was now in a mercer's
shop at Ipswich. He frequently came to see his
sisters, and, as we were about the same age, our
boyish acquaintance was renewed and ripened into
sincere friendship.

> When friend meets friend, how time glides on !
> How swiftly steal the hours away !
> The heart forgets each tiny care,
> And warmly beats with bounding play;
> The sparkling eye, and cheerful brow,
> And beaming smile that hour attend—
> That happy hour of social joys,
> The happy hour when friend meets friend.
>
> The blackbird loves the close of day;
> The skylark loves the morning dawn;
> The nightingale the hour loves best
> When other birds to sleep are gone;
> The schoolboy loves the hour of play;
> The swain the hour his labours end;
> But oh ! give me that happy hour,
> The happy hour when friend meets friend.

My friend Alfred Bowman and I were somewhat
similar in our tastes and pursuits, and when he was
away we carried on a frequent correspondence. We

compared and corrected for each other our efforts
in rhyme, exchanged sentiments on distinguished
authors, and thus derived mutual instruction, and
improved ourselves in the art of composition.

I wrote several minor pieces about this time, one
of which I have preserved. It is as follows.   I
must, however, premise that this poem, and others
which I may hereafter insert, have received cor-
rections more or less since they were first written.

ON MY FIRST GREY HAIR.*

The mossy well, the trembling tower,
The rainbow through the misty shower,
The autumn's drooping, withering flower,
    All alike this truth display,
    Art and Nature's works decay.

This silvery hair, untimely guest,
Like snow upon the summer's breast,
Awakes in me sad interest.
    While I gaze it seems to say :
    Man must also pass away.

Since, then, proud towers, by Time decayed,
Must bow to earth ; all nature fade ;
And man must in the grave be laid,
    Reason and Religion say :
    Prepare for an eternal day.

Fifth Month 6th, 1825.

---

* His hair began to turn grey about the age of sixteen.

FROM GRAVE TO GAY.

Some centuries ago, in the days of the fairies,
When monarchs indulged in the strangest vagaries,
And people did likewise, there lived an odd king,
Whose whims and whose ways I am going to sing.
There never was seen such a comical fellow,
He dressed in all colours, blue, purple, and yellow.
Now he sailed in the air, now rode in a carriage,
For whatever he did he could not disparage
His title or fame.   This seems strange in your sight,
But *his* doing a thing made it proper and right.
His power was despotic o'er his whole jurisdiction,
Yet his people had for him a strange predilection.
For whatever he ordered, however outrageous,
Was promptly obeyed by all sexes and ages ;
And once he commanded, as a stretch of his might,
Folks should sleep in the day and be up all the night.
This made them all wonder, yet glad to obey,
They crept out at midnight, and snored all the day.
He made many such laws, which I need not here mention,
Because to repeat them would be a detention.
But if he had ordered that all who perambulate,
Each, instead of his ten toes, should walk on his pate,
I suppose that the folks would have quickly obeyed,
And each tottered forth on his hands and his head.
Though so strange in his ways, yet by all he was loved,
At least he was followed, though by some not approved.
But admired or not, he had little to fear,
Since the loudest against him trod close in his rear.
By two things he was known ; he was partial to ladies ;
And to please any whim never cared about pay-days.
        I have finished my picture, and faithfully dressed him.
Some, perhaps, from this sketch will be fit to detest him,

Will be anxious at least to be told of his name,
Ere they laugh at his whims or incautiously blame.
Then I'll say what they call this droll king of the nation
His *real* name is Folly, his *true* name is Fashion.

STANZA.

How sweet is night, and sweet night's blushing Queen
As forth she moves majestic, calm and slow,
Augustly riding o'er the blue serene,
And gilding nature with a tranquil glow !
How breathlessly the wide world sleeps below !
Clouds 'neath her path in rugged grandeur lie,
Like mountains crowned with everlasting snow,
While stars hang forth their torches in the sky,
And strew their pearly beams o'er heaven's broad canopy.

HOPE.

Look at her cheerful brow,
Her locks that lightly on her shoulders lie,
Her mantle dipp'd in snow,
And the quick lustre of her dark blue eye.

Hope ! lovely maid divine !
Delusive tho' the world may say thou art,
Thee I will ne'er resign,
Thou sweet consoler of the woe-worn heart.

The fields with flowers array'd
Exult in beauty only for awhile ;
But thou, delightful maid,
Alike all seasons, thou dost ever smile.

I'll call thee, then, mine own
Hope ! thou young wanderer from the starry skies;
Come, make my breast thy throne,
And when I weep wipe thou my tearful eyes.

The principal part of my spare time I continued to devote to the correction of an epic poem. But when I had gone through about half of it, a change came over me which put a stop to my labours. Strong religious convictions possessed me that it would be wrong for me to proceed in this employment. These convictions, I believe, in part arose from the circumstance of a religious visit which was paid to us by my former schoolmaster, William Impey, a devout man, who was a minister in the Society. In his communication to me he laid great stress on the necessity of my giving up my " delectable things," in order to obtain divine favour. After much reflection, I came to the conclusion that it was wrong for me to employ my time in the composition of a poem which related events as facts which, in truth, never took place. Under this impression I felt it to be my duty to destroy my poem, and I therefore burnt it, only reserving a table of its contents and a few extracts, which I thought might prove of service at some future time. This was a severe trial of principle to me, for I doted much on my epic. But though I have since come to the belief that the argument against the use of fiction is not in all cases to be maintained, and though, in this particular instance, I consider that it was not sufficient, seeing that the poem was intended to illustrate that great moral, the impolicy of war, yet I have never regretted that I made the sacrifice, for this simple reason, that I believed it at the time to be a point of duty. In future, if I be ambitious, let it be to do good, and if I be honoured, let it be for the good that I have done.

Whilst I was thus versifying with an industry

and ardour which few could surpass, my thoughts
and feelings were agitated by passing events, which
deeply affected my enjoyments.

The family of the Bowmans, with whom we were
so intimate and for whom we entertained such a
sincere friendship, gave up housekeeping this summer, and left Kelvedon.

Perhaps I may as well in this place anticipate
the future, and relate the short remaining history
of Martha Bowman, my especial friend. She married
Benjamin Donbavand, of Pontefract, had one child,
and, shortly afterwards, died of consumption. Her
husband, in about a year, followed her to the grave.
I did not hear of the death of my lamented friend till
the day of her funeral. I lay awake that night and
composed the following verses on the melancholy
event.

LINES ON THE DEATH OF MARTHA.

The canopy of night is flung far over earth and sky,
And here and there a lonely star gleams faintly from on
     high ;   [north,
The sullen clouds, in many a fold, hang o'er the gloomy
And winds from their unknown abodes come wildly
     whistling forth.

This midnight hour will I consign to grief for one no more,
Whom once I knew, as well as loved, in days that now are
     o'er,
In years when pleasures circled me, and flowers my path
     o'erspread,
And day-dreams of delight were mine that with those
     years are fled.

They tell me she has died, oh, yes ! they tell me she has
 died,
That gentle one who oftentimes has wandered by my
 side,
Who often has admired with me, in days and years gone by,
The hill and vale, the moon and stars, the pomp of earth
 and sky.

To-night, to-night, the chilly earth is her untimely bed,
The curtains of the grave, alas ! are drawn around her
 head,
And those illumined eyes are quenched, that sparkled
 once with glee,
And hushed are those expressive lips whose music flowed
 for me.

Oh spirit ! wheresoe'er thou art, the object of my love,
Whether thou wing'st thy way unseen to happy realms
 above,
Or walk'st the courts of heavenly bliss, or sit'st in sacred
 bowers,
Where angels wreath their holy harps with amaranthine
 flowers ;

Or whether, as a guardian saint, thou flittest here unseen,
And visitest thy favourite spot and scenes where thou hast
 been,
Or dwell'st in one of yon bright stars, those stars which
 we have guessed
Might be, perchance, the sweet abodes and mansions of
 the blest ;

I know thou wear'st a crown of bliss wherever thou
 may'st be,
For crowns of bliss to those are given who live and die
 like thee ;

But I shall mourn while others laugh, and sigh among
     the glad,
To think these eyes no more shall greet the friend that
     once I had.

Here let me pause a moment, while I take a parting glance at the compositions of my early days.
They give, I acknowledge, but little promise of
future excellence; but to those who love to trace the
current of the mind they will not be without interest.
It may be observed that many of them are serious in
their character.   My mind, in truth, was deeply
imbued with religious principles.   My spirit panted
to get free from the thraldom of human nature, and
luxuriate, as it were, amidst the holy and the pure.
I was ambitious of distinction, but I earnestly desired
to render this passion of my mind subordinate to the
superior concernment of a preparation for a future
state of being; and, as such a passion was infused
into my nature, I sought to direct it into worthy
channels, and to make it subservient to noble pur-
poses.

A subject which deeply engaged our thoughts at
this time was the declining health of my sister Ann.
It was evident to all her friends, although we ourselves could hardly see it, that she was gradually
sinking in a consumption.   I frequently took her a
little drive; but neither this, nor the prescriptions of
her doctors, arrested the progress of her lingering
complaint.

On the night of the 6th of the Second Month my
father came to summon my brother and myself to her

death-bed. My sister was quite sensible, but a great change had come over her. She, whose lips were so unused to speak on the subject of religion, whose piety, like a vestal flame, burnt secretly in the sanctuary of her own heart, now, on the verge of the eternal world, cast aside her natural reserve, and opened her dying lips in devout ejaculations, and, in sacred humility, put up her last prayers to the great Author of her existence, before whom she was about to appear.

The awfulness of a death-bed scene is a reality in a world of shadows which experience alone can make men comprehend.

Many and bitter were the tears which I shed that memorable night.

Sometimes her spirit seemed already to have entered on the fruition of heavenly joy. "Oh eternity!" she whispered, "Eternity, what is it?" "I fancy I hear the sound of music—not earthly music." "Oh how delightful to sink to glory!"

Having repeatedly bade us farewell, she at length once more sweetly said, "Farewell all;" then closing her eyes she lay still as if she were falling into a peaceful slumber. A solemn silence intervened for about a quarter of an hour, and then her spirit gently passed away.

The funeral took place at Kelvedon on St. Valentine's day, and the attendance was large. The snow fell heavily on the coffin as we stood round the grave of my sister, and a prayer arose in my heart that my end might be as peaceful as hers, and my portion in the world to come as glorious.

MY SISTERS.

I had two sisters in my youth,
Before I knew their worth and truth—
Lucy and Ann.   Early they died,
But not unloved, unwept, unsighed.
But those that loved, wept, sighed, alas !
Mostly, like them, sleep 'neath the grass.
My mother, chief of all, whose heart
Ceased never to endure the smart,
Till death drew nigh, his seal to place
On her so fair angelic face.
    From one paternal stock they came,
Their early nurture was the same,
And yet they were unlike.   Their lot
Was cast together in one spot ;
Both nestled softly in one bed,
Both from one porridge-bowl were fed,
Both heard one clock proclaim the hours,
Both grew amidst the self-same flowers ;
Yet Nature—gay, capricious, bold—
Fashioned them in a different mould,
In form and character and mind.
Nature is wise, 'tis we are blind.
But there was mystery deeper still,
A mystery woven, as with skill,
Into the tissue of their fate
Which who shall solve ? For, strange to state,
The maladies from which they died,
These two anomalies supplied.
Each was the contrast, in its course,
Of her who sank beneath its force.
A strange and marked antithesis
Twixt life and death was surely this.

But though their deaths had each this type,
Yet both alike for heaven were ripe.
  My sister Lucy was "a mild,
A sweet, engaging, charming child; "
And thus she grew to full seventeen,
A tall meek girl of gentle mien.
Oval and shapely was her face,
Of rosy brown, in which the grace
Of thoughtfulness prevailed. Her eyes
Were hazel, wherein beauty lies ;
Her voice was rich, distinct and slow,
Coming from tranquil depths. We know
Voices, like faces, never match;
But both possess the power to catch
And fascinate the observer's heart,
And hers succeeded without art.
As flowers exhale their perfumes, so
A sense of goodness seemed to flow
As from her presence ; and she stood
Erect, the rose of maidenhood.
All but for one small fault or foil,
For faults like hers improve —not spoil.
Her dark hair was of curlless grain,
Inflexibly, yet meekly plain,
The type of an enduring will,
Of suffering, yet of conquering still.
  The times were adverse. Wasteful wars,
Harsh Government, restrictive laws,
Had crushed the springs of trade. Around
Seditious cries burst from the ground ;
And hungry men, and women too,
Were both mowed down on Peterloo.
Like many more our little band
Launched forth to seek a happier land

Across the unmeasured sea.   Our helm
Towards Washington's enfranchised realm,
Guided our bark.   Erelong we found
A shore with peace and plenty crowned,
The breastwork of a mighty sea
Formed to be free—and to set free;
An empire rising from the main,
Like a young eagle from the plain,
And soaring Westward!   In that land
We found the stranger's helping hand
And loving heart—but not a home.
They who to distant regions roam
Alone can tell, midst fairest scenes,
All that the word " home-sickness " means.
    We dwelt beside the Delaware,
The broad and surging Delaware,
Where ships from England stemmed the tide
In flying jib and topsail pride,
Bringing the news from distant parts,
And love from long-divided hearts.
    The Indian summer, with its calm
And hazy air, and breathing balm—
A sylvan carnival—the old
And sober forests dressed in gold,
Purple and saffron—all had passed,
And idle winter came at last,
Freakish, and full of uncouth play,
Acting the chandler on his way.
Keen was the cold; while from some high
And temperate region of the sky,
The rain came down, and, as it fell,
It froze as by some mystic spell,
Whate'er it touched, converted it
Into a diamond tissue, fit

For fairy palace, bright, but cold ;
The house, the barn, the forest old,
Were cased in ice !   Each tiny twig
Grew, with the slow accretion, big ;
The leafless, yet o'erladen trees,
Surging and swaying in the breeze,
Bent their proud heads.   Even the oak
Beheld his limbs bowed down and broke.
The horseman in the forest drear,
When the wind rose, beheld with fear
The ponderous boughs, with crashing sound,
Hurled bright and shivering to the ground ;
And spurred his steed to quit with haste,
The precincts of the spectral waste.
    While thus the Frost-king fixed his hold
On flood and field, on wood and wold,
Our Lucy faced a sterner king !
She lived just long enough to bring
Admirers round her, though perchance
Unconscious of the admiring glance.
And then we lost her !   Her complaint
Was raging fever.   She, the saint
Of more than human meekness, fell
Beneath the furious scourge.   How well
Do I remember—yes, e'en now—
Her burning cheek and anguished brow.
Yet was her pure and tranquil mind
Alike to life or death resigned.
'Twas for her mother's sake alone
She wished to live—not for her own.
    Two kings strove o'er her day and night,—
The Frost-king, armed with direful might,
Into her very chamber came,
Despite the wood-fire's potent flame ;

But though thus fiercely he assailed,
The King of Terrors, *He* prevailed !
    A group of loving friends stood round
Her mean, uncurtained bed. No sound
Was heard ; but every tearful eye
Was fixed on her. We watched her die
Gently—unconsciously—as though
A bubbling brook had ceased to flow !
And when her spirit was dismissed,
Her moveless lips we stooped and kissed.
    A winding sheet of snow was spread
O'er nature, when to her last bed
Lucy was borne—an emblem just
Of her who now returned to dust.
    She sleeps beside the Delaware,
The broad and surging Delaware !
Whence ships to England speed their way,
With gallant hearts and streamers gay.
But she, whose grave is on that shore,
May see her native land no more !
    Younger by four revolving years
Than Lucy—child of smiles and tears—
Was my fair sister Ann ; a girl
Unfit for life's unfeeling whirl ;
Of temper quick, and yet a maid
Of Spartan courage, not afraid
To go at evening-hour alone,
When a mere child, to bring a bone
From the dim charnel-house that stood
Behind the village church. The wood
The flowery fields, she loved to pace ;
None could outstrip her at a race ;
And, in that distant foreign land,
Barefoot, amidst the burning sand,

She wandered wild ; or on the mead
Captured and rode the unsaddled steed.
She lavished many tender thoughts
On animals of various sorts.
She tamed them with instinctive skill,
And made them docile to her will.
But bards and heroes most of all
Held her romantic mind in thrall.
Once with another laughing elf
(Doomed to die early like herself)
She sought the fortune-teller's door
To profit by her mystic lore.
She promised her a Valentine.
Too true, O, Grave ! for she was thine !

　　With years and growth there also came
Development of mental frame;
And impulses for good or ill
Strove for the mastery of her will.
Fierce wars disturbed her inner life ;
But goodness triumphed in the strife.

　　Five changeful years elapsed.　Again
Homewards across the Atlantic main
Midst howling storms our course we bore,
Quitting that friendly, foreign shore
With many fond regrets.　We left
·While wood and field were still bereft,
By winter's long protracted sway,
Of every tinge of green.　O, day
Of rapture ! day of pure delight !
At last old England blessed our sight,
Clothed in that flush that summer yields
Of emerald beauty—with the fields
Golden with buttercups—and trees
Waving their young leaves in the breeze,

G

While merry skylarks, on the wing,
" Welcome to England ! " seemed to sing.
   Near by the German Ocean's shore,
Amidst her childhood's scenes once more,
New modes of life, new trains of thought
Their changes in my sister wrought.
Modelling herself by those around
Her proper bearing soon she found.
Her vaulting spirit sought to soar
As high as others.   In the lore
Of books she feasted.   Science drew
Her feet fresh labyrinths to pursue.
And thus, ere long, a woman grown,
Amongst the fairest forth she shone
Perfect in symmetry.   Not tall,
But round of form.   Her head was small
But firmly set upon her fair
And graceful neck.   Her auburn hair
Flowed in luxuriant folds.   Her face
Was pale, as of the lily race.
   Romantic girl, too soon she found
The path she trod was hollow ground ;
That life was not what fancy told !—
That all that glittered was not gold !—
Ardent, true-hearted, soon she learned
That one, o'er whom her soul had yearned—
A female friend of brilliant powers—
The confidante of social hours—
Full of professions of regard—
Was false at heart !   The blow struck hard.
My sister's soul, thus rudely woke,
Recoiled within her at the stroke.
Her eyes were opened !   She beheld
Life's first illusive charm dispelled.

But deep the wound within remained,
And nature's vital chords were strained.
  Her soul's capacity of love
And joy were boundless ; far above
That of inferior natures. Hope
Illumed her fancy's wildest scope ;
But actual life fell sorely short
Of her ideal standard. Nought
Could soothe her breast. The fiery strife
Burnt inwardly the thread of life.—
Or was it that some secret flame
Of unrequited love o'ercame
Her proud young spirit ? Did she sigh
Over some idol of her eye
In lonely grief ? Perhaps she did !—
Too oft the fondest love is hid.
  Her health gave way. A slow decline
Seemed her young strength to undermine.
As when a veteran chief sits down
Before some coveted fair town,
So does Consumption, with like skill,
Besiege his victim. Patient still,
But persevering, day by day,
And month by month, he works his way
By sap and mine and slow approach,
Nearer and nearer to encroach ;
Uses each art of feint and fence,
With vain illusions lulls each sense,
Cuts off supplies of vital strength,
And captures by surprise at length.
  Thus sank my sister by this slow,
This sure, but most delusive foe.
" Better," still " better "—she would say,
Yet growing weaker day by day,

And laying plans for future years,
As if to banish others' fears.
  Fond of the dumb creation still,
An aged friend, with kind good will,
Gave her a little kitten, lithe
As india-rubber, and as blithe
As blithest lambkin of the field;
Much pleasure did its antics yield
To my poor sister: and she nursed
The little beauty with a burst
Of mother's love. She watched it play
With ceaseless interest every day.
It served her fancy to beguile
And sometimes won a happy smile.
  Thus, month by month, she sank. 'Twas strange
To mark the sure, but gradual, change
Wrought in her spirit, once so high;
And yet the brightness of her eye.
Grew more intense. Sometimes the strife
Of feelings in her inner life
Dissolved her into tears. Then peace
Would follow, and the conflict cease.
Disease dealt gently with her. Bland
The touches of the spoiler's hand!
In wisdom fitted to subdue
Her rebel nature, and renew
A childlike spirit. No complaint
Was uttered by the dying saint;
But to her face each day was given
Still less of earth—still more of Heaven.
  At length the midnight hour drew nigh
When my sweet sister Ann must die.
We gathered round her. She was calm
As though reposing on an Arm

Divine! And now her lips in prayer
And praise were opened. All the air
Was holy in her presence. Love
And joy o'erflowed her from above !
Nothing stood in her way. She thought
Her ears the songs of angels caught.
"O ! how delightful is it thus
To sink to glory !" So, to us,
She with the voice of triumph cried.—
Her brothers kneeling by her side,
Upon her elder brother's head
(He, too, alas ! long since is dead)
She placed her hand—then on my own—
And called down blessings from the Throne
Of Heaven upon us. Strange to think,
Though on Eternity's dread brink,
She did not, at that hour, forget
Her young and playful little pet ;
But made us promise we would take
Care of her favourite for her sake !
Then, bidding us farewell, she lay
As if asleep ; and passed away
In peace. The waft of death was mild
As Zephyr playing with a child !
    There is one short month in ev'ry year
Of which the fourteenth day is dear
To every female heart. But I
Welcome it ever with a sigh,
For on that day the Grave held wide
His arms to claim his beauteous bride.
Her marriage wreath was driven snow.
Tears at a wedding sometimes flow ;
And many tears were shed that day
When our fair bride was given away.

Thus, at the age of twenty-two
Short years—her lease of life run through—
Our Ann we lost; a great, a glad,
A glorious change *for her*; a sad
And ceaseless loss to those she left
Behind, of household light bereft.
But all is doubtless for the best
That she is gone to endless rest!
Me duty calls still to *endure*;
And duty's recompense is sure.

CHAPTER VII.

Removal to Colchester—Reflections on attaining his majority
—" Ambition " — Non-resistance : an anecdote — Book
Society—Poem on his friend Alfred Bowman, entitled
" Arthur and Helen."

On the 25th of Third Month, 1828, my father
having hired some premises at Colchester for a
brewery, our little family, which consisted now of
only four, once again left Kelvedon, to begin the
world anew.

There was one thing belonging to our new residence which particularly pleased me. At the back
of the house there was a little upstairs room which
overlooked the garden. To this room I laid claim.
I made it my little castle, to which I could resort at
all times, and find a quiet shelter from the harassing
cares of life. Here I placed my secretaire, containing
my writing ammunition and all my manuscript treasures. I suspended some shelves for my few beloved
books, and round the whitewashed walls of my
room I nailed up pictures and engravings of the
most motley description, and called it my picture
room.

It happened very singularly that only a few days
before we left Kelvedon I received a letter from our
old companion in adventures, Christopher Stopes.
After a consultation among ourselves we concluded
that it would be very desirable to have his services

in our new employment. We accordingly sent him
proposals which he at once accepted; and, in the
course of the following month, he once more came
and took up his abode under our roof.

The 3rd of Third Month, 1829 at length arrived,
and I found myself of age.

REFLECTIONS ON COMING OF AGE.

"I have now been twenty-one years an inhabitant of earth. I look back and perceive that the
gates of boyhood are closed upon me for ever. During these twenty-one years I have undergone many
tribulations; and I have also enjoyed many pleasures. I have been in the Old World and I have
been in the New World. I have known what it is
to be in danger of losing my life both on land and at
sea. I have seen much of men, and of the ways of
men. And now, at the age of twenty-one years, I
look around me with a somewhat experienced eye.

"Hope is pointing out to me prospective pleasures,
permanent in their nature, and unalloyed in their
composition; but I know that her promises are
fallacious. Fancy, too, is inviting me to her flowery
vales; but I know full well that they are all ideal.
I see that virtue is, beyond all controversy, the
greatest treasure here on earth, and that the attainment of a life of immortal bliss in Heaven is of all
things most worthy the concern of a soul immortal."

The passions of men, it appears to me, were
implanted in the human constitution for good pur-
poses. They were implanted by the Divine Being,

and all that He does is good. It is the duty and a
part of the great business of man to regulate and
govern these passions, and to turn them to their
proper account. What I mean is that his love
should be directed to that which is virtuous—his
hate to the hatred of that which is wicked—his
covetousness to the possession of that which is
really valuable—and his ambition to the attainment,
of the purest glory.

AMBITION.

What racking thoughts disturb my mind !
  What visions cheat my eyes !
I long to leave the gloom behind !
  I long aloft to rise.

How boundless are the soul's desires !
  How far her aims extend !
Still on the wing she never tires,
  Nor finds her journey's end.

I long to take my stand with you,
  Ye dazzling sons of Fame !
To drink the unsullied ether's blue,
  And share the world's acclaim !

I long the mountain top to climb !
  Stand on its crown of snow !
And shout on any crag sublime,
  Where others dare not go.

And there, with eager arms outspread,
  Reach darkling into space ;
Talk with the spirits of the dead,
  And bards of old embrace.

In dreams like these e'en life and love,
  Unheeded, are forgot;
The earth beneath—the world above—
  And e'en my humble lot.

To others on oblivion's deep,
  Let wealth and power be given;
Mine be the hand the harp to sweep!
  The eye to reach to Heaven!

Eleventh Month 27th, 1830.—With regard to myself and my affairs, being now in the twenty-third year of my age, I am taking a great deal of interest in politics and literature.

Twelfth Month 1st, 1830.—Went up in the evening to see ——. Talked politics. Told me of great disturbances at Alton. Many of the inhabitants made special constables. We then discussed how far the principles of non-resistance, arising from a trust in an all-protecting Providence, would secure a man in times of popular commotion.

I related an anecdote of a family in the back settlements of America. The Indians were at war with the Americans. A man one day perceived a party of Indians approaching his house. His wife and family were with him indoors. What was to be done? He expected they would be tomahawked, and the house burnt to the ground. He immediately opened the door, extended his hand to the chief of the party, and invited the whole of them in. They were astonished. He and his wife produced what provisions they had in the house, and treated the party with respectful hospitality. After having regaled themselves, and, I think, returned thanks to their host, they peaceably withdrew. They had not gone far, however, when the chief ran back, and pulling a feather out of his cap, stuck it over the door as a sign to another party who were foraging in the neighbourhood, and might perhaps come there, that they should spare that house.

First Month 5th, 1831.—Monthly Meeting. Some friends to dinner. Discussed the subject of forming a Book Society. Several of us met at William R. Dell's in the evening, and agreed upon the principal features of the Society, and drew up some primary rules accordingly. These we signed. Having more time than most of the other members, and taking a great interest in its prosperity, the management of the Society soon devolved chiefly on myself. I became, in short, its Librarian, Treasurer, and Secretary.

The many new and interesting publications which it introduced to my notice greatly enlarged my knowledge, and made me acquainted with the literary character of the age. Hitherto my reading had principally been among a departed school of authors, and I had imbibed a strong prejudice against the moderns; but now I saw some of the periodicals in which, though I met with much that did violence to my taste, yet I also found a great deal that served to stimulate my mind and induce me to exert myself to work out my way, if possible, to excellence.

Our town was visited this summer (1834) by that

fearful pestilence, the cholera.   It commenced its
ravages in Asia, and proceeded westward in its deadly
march around the globe.   On its arrival in England
we were greatly alarmed. Nervous people, especially,
were dreadfully afraid of its approach.

The ravages of the cholera were principally among
the poor and the intemperate, and many very affecting
cases occurred.   It was particularly dismal to hear
the constant tolling of the funeral bell.   I remember
on one occasion being struck with the sight of a
passing funeral where there was not even one solitary
mourner to follow the coffin to its resting-place—
neither father, nor sister, nor child !   It seemed to
me to show the fearful character of the pestilence
more than anything else that came under my
notice.

It may not be uninteresting to mention that, during
the time when the pestilence was prevalent, the phe-
nomenon occurred of a remarkable flight of insects.
Millions of billions filled the air, over, I believe, the
whole extent of the country.   They were very small
in size, but their wings were large in proportion ; and
from east to west they continued their silent flight,
without cessation or diminution, for weeks together.

Tenth Month 7th.—Died, at Bardfield, about five
o'clock in the morning, my dear, congenial friend
and correspondent Alfred Bowman.   Although I
have before mentioned the name of this estimable
young man, yet I have refrained from dwelling much
on the subject of our friendship, as I have related the
particulars of it in the following poem, under the
fictitious names of—

ARTHUR AND HELEN.

They say that men are faithless. O! there are
Whose hearts are steadfast as the polar star;
Beings whose love—deep, tender, and sublime—
Can outlive hope, and triumph over time;
Who, if the objects of their fondness cease
To love in turn, through coldness or caprice,
Can still love on, can every ill forgive,
Forego new joys, and on remembrance live;
Clasp to their breasts the visionary dove,
And die the victims of devoted love.
    In youth's warm spring-time generous thoughts impart
A glow to life; and warm was Arthur's heart.
Within his breast no seeming mystery dwelt
O'er which Conjecture and Suspicion spelt;
But all was frankness there: no dark disguise
Veiled up his character from curious eyes;
The look of candour which his countenance wore
Might move less interest, but it pleased the more.
His form was handsome, though his frame was weak,
A sickly paleness dwelt upon his cheek;
But o'er his manly face that sickly hue
An air of Heaven—a charm of beauty threw.
Around his lips the eye his soul could trace,
And sunshine seemed reflected from his face.
His voice was liquid and his words flowed fast,
And sweetly trembled as his lips they passed.
He spoke without reserve and spoke with sense,
And reasoned well when driven to defence.
But chiefly he was wont in woman's ear
To pour the eloquence she loves to hear.
He made acquaintance soon with every child:
They looked up at him, trusted him, and smiled;

Forgot their little fears and first alarms,
And ran, confiding, to his clasping arms.
Much had he read, but yet he studied not;
And what is idly read is soon forgot;
Still, much he knew; and what he knew was worth
More than much knowledge which, in nooks of earth,
Dull schoolmen prize. The wisdom which he drank
Was not drawn up from Learning's leaden tank,
He quenched his thirst at Nature's crystal rills,
And sipped the dew-drops which the morn distils.
The song of birds, the wind's majestic roar,
The solemn fall of billows on the shore.
Nature has many tongues with which to teach;
He knew them all, and comprehended each;
And when he looked on earth or gazed on high,
And saw the planets navigate the sky,
Mind, with her various powers, within him wrought
And furnished soon his treasury of thought.
He saw ideal forms all pure and bright,
And peopled earth with denizens of light.
Exalted thus above the mean and base
He shunned the frigid of the human race.
He was not proud, and yet he could despise
Ignoble minds that never dare to rise.
He loved the bards: he loved to feel their power
Come o'er his spirit in the lonely hour.
Nor was this all: his feelings warm and strong
He too poured forth in animated song.
Music and song his spirit seemed to suit,
Sweetly he blew the mellow-sounding flute.
His pencil, too, he used with pleasing skill,
And called forth forms of loveliness at will.
Not stern of soul, nor muscular of form,
He was not made to buffet with the storm.

But sensitive alike of joy or woe,
Feelings were his which only poets know.
His conscientious eye was clear and strong,
Detecting what was right and what was wrong;
He spurned the wrong and sided with the right,
And kept the tendency of things in sight.
No fierce defender of his favourite cause,
He knew society and owned its laws;
In manhood, still partaking of the child,
His mind was active, and his manners mild;
This gave a charm to all he said or did;
But half his worth within his breast he hid.
    And we were friends. From boyhood we were friends :
How sweet a charm the recollection lends!
But we were sundered soon. He bent his way
To Caledonia's lakes and mountains gray,
New scenes to him! And there he tarried long.
He loved the land of battles and of song.
It suited well his taste. But as for me
My lot was cast upon the boisterous sea,
To ride a puny bark with masts and sails,
The sport of waves, the plaything of the gales;
To suffer hardships in a foreign clime,
(Exiled from home, though guiltless of a crime,)
Recall my native land—though distant, dear—
And soothe my grief with many a boyish tear.
Long time elapsed. At length my foot I set
Once more on Albion's isle. Again we met.
But both were changed. To opening manhood grown
Our characters had each acquired its tone;
His had received that polish which we find
Mixing with men bestows upon mankind;
My own the stormy fretfulness of those
Who roam the world, but never find repose.

And yet we were alike in one respect,
This saved our friendship, else it had been wreck'd.
One bent we had—in both the love was strong—
The ardent love of spirit-stirring song.
We talked of bards of old whom each admired,
Whose music pleased us and whose genius fired;
And while we passed their merits in review,
Unnoticed by ourselves, our friendship grew.
　　We dwelt apart.   How oft it happens here
They dwell the farthest off we would were near.
We dwelt apart; yet sometimes met, and when
Placed at a distance we employed the pen.
We wrote of many, many things; sometimes
We sent each other our precocious rhymes
To mend and smooth, for in my humble way
I, too, could frame the pleasant sounding lay.
Thus rolled Time's onward flood, and still it bore
Sweet gems and shining shells to Friendship's shore.
　　And now at length my friend attained the age
To act his part on manhood's busy stage;
To share its ceaseless toil, its 'wildering strife,
And feel the sweet solicitudes of life.
His future path lay pleasant to the sight,
His hopes were buoyant, and his sky was bright.
Fond of society, a friendship grew
Between young Arthur and a chosen few.
And one he loved.   She seemed to Arthur's eyes
Some beauteous emanation from the skies;
Or dream embodied; such as dance around
The brows of bards in pleasing slumbers bound.
Her form was slight, her step was full of grace,
And gentleness was pictured on her face.
Pale was her dimpled cheek; her dark brown hair
Hung curling down her neck and nestled there.

She wore a meek reserve; and though her heart
Had warm affections, yet it had no part
In those more passionate and hidden fires
Which live in some hearts when all else expires.
Her character was not like his, yet still
He loved her, in defiance of his will;
For love exerts a strange, tyrannic might,
And bids the most dissimilar unite;
Glows with the fervour of the noon-day sun,
And melts discordant natures into one.
Music was her delight, and when, to please
Young Arthur, she would sweep the ivory keys
With her white fingers, and, with varying voice,
Now mourn with pity, now with hope rejoice,
And turn and fix her large bright eyes on him,
His limbs would tremble and his sight grow dim.
    And Helen loved young Arthur: and they two
Were happy in each other's love; for who
Can feel confided in, and can confide,
Share the sweet sympathy of hearts allied,
Partake the dear and unreproved caress,
Feel heaven expand above and earth grow less,
And not be happy?—Happier than the morn
When the lark greets her with his silver horn.
O! youthful love! how exquisite thou art!
Thou fill'st with joy that little world, the heart;
And, with thy presence and thy magic powers,
Turnest the desert to a land of flowers;
Throwest a halo round all earthly things,
And fannest fragrance from thy downy wings!
A rumour reached my ear. I heard it said
That Arthur—that my friend—would shortly wed.
I own these tidings took me by surprise;
This may seem strange. But I must not disguise

H

That now he seldom wrote.   Yet I inferred
No change in him because I seldom heard ;
On such neglect I laid but little stress,
I knew his heart and knew it loved not less.
The world's engrossing cares, I knew full well,
Had bound him with a strong enthralling spell,
And so I was content : and when I learned
This startling news, my heart within me burned,
The Past rolled back upon me like a tide,
While Hope a bright futurity supplied.
My spirit rose, my thoughts began to chime,
And soon I wrote, in sprightly Scottish rhyme,
A long and quaint epistle, which I sent,
To show my interest in the great event.
Arthur had promised, in his warmth of heart,
Long since, some effort of his pencilling art ;
This promise now I pressed him to fulfil ;
I wished for some such effort of his skill
To grace my picture-room, that when long miles
Deprived me of his cheerful voice and smiles
It might recall, whene'er it met mine eye,
The friend I loved.   He wrote me no reply.

    Erelong another rumour reached my ear—
A vague report that o'er my friend's career
A storm had burst, and all his prospects—all
His gilded hopes were buried in one fall !
    Again we met.   My friend, I ought to say,
Had relatives who dwelt not far away ;
'Twas there we met.   I found him still the same,
His face all smiles, his eyes a lambent flame.
The whirlwind that had laid his fortunes low,
Had changed him not, nor touched his brow with woe ;
But like the bulrush, bent beneath the blast,
He rose uninjured when the storm was past :

For though his frame was weak, and though his face
Showed not the firmness of the Stoic race,
His was the innocent, elastic mind,
Which soon rebounding, leaves its cares behind.
The hour arrived, and Arthur left the place
Where shone no sun for him but one dear face!
O'er that last hour let darkness spread its wings,
And be it buried with forgotten things.
They who have known what partings are, can tell
All that lies hid beneath that word—Farewell!
He left the place, and reached another scene;
The weary breadth of England lay between:
But, like himself, where'er he chanced to roam,
He made at once his new abode—a home.
Her love he still possessed whose love could throw
A light around him and assuage his woe;
And letters passed—that medium which supplies
The absent voices of the lips and eyes;
Brings separated friends and lovers near,
And whispers secrets in a distant ear.
And Arthur's heart was social, and he found
Companions soon, with whom to gather round
The cheerful evening fire, and talk, and play
With children like himself—as was his way.
And he seemed happy, though a pensive sigh
Would now and then his cheerfulness belie:
For Helen's image—beauteous, gentle, kind—
Haunted from day to day his secret mind;
And when he left the circle where he shone
An hour before, and found himself alone,
It was to feel more sensibly the smart
Of hopeless love still rankling at his heart.
And then his troubled spirit would repine,
And he would ask why feelings all too fine—

Too exquisitely fine—disturbed his breast,
Which others knew not of, and so were blest.
But soon the thought would tranquillise his mind,
That all his sorrows, doubtless, were designed
To render him more humble, and more prone
To place his trust in Providence alone.
And he would pray to have his inmost heart
Made calm, and pure, and more from earth apart.
   I said that Arthur found new friends; but yet
'Twas not in him his old ones to forget,
For whom (to use his words) his life-blood still
Boiled through his veins : and he would sometimes fill
The friendly page, to tell me how he fared,
And have his pleasures and his sorrows shared.
The promise, too, which he in days long passed
Had kindly made, he now fulfilled at last,
And sent a sketch to illustrate First Love—
A young girl clasping to her breast a dove.
Yes! there she is, in all her youthful charms,
Pressing the gentle bird within her arms !
O! never, never, can I gaze on her,
And not to thee, my faithful friend, recur!
   Time rolled away, and once again we met—
It was in Spring; and ere the sun had set,
We wandered forth, on nature's face to gaze,
And talk, as we were wont in former days.
Down a green lane we turned, an English lane !—
What is so lovely as an English lane ?—
With shady oaks and elms on either side,
Spreading their boughs the calm retreat to hide ;
Delicious banks, where young herbs lift their heads,
And velvet mosses make their fairy beds ;
And there a bright and ever-gurgling brook,
Where the sweet primrose peeps from every nook,

Tempting the children of the hamlet near
With many a wish, subdued by many a fear.
While thus we rambled carelessly along,
We talked by turns of science and of song;
Of woman, too !—a theme in which his heart
Was wont to take an animated part.
Woman! that theme of which men ne'er grow tired—
That theme on which the dullest are inspired !
I spoke of Helen, who, as yet, was known
To me by little more than name alone ;
For in his letters never would he dwell
On that one subject—why, I could not tell.
I knew not then that Helen had enchained
His inmost heart, and o'er his bosom reigned.
He made one brief remark : he said that he
Was bound himself, but that he left her free.

 We parted ; and my friend returned, again
To hide with outward smiles his inward pain,
And trust the future for that happier lot
Which present time, alas ! accorded not.

 Another storm, severer than the first,
Was gathering round young Arthur, soon to burst.
His own First Love—his Helen—she on whom
His heart and hope depended—she on whom
His very life was staked—his all on earth—
His darling choice—his only gem of worth—
Left him ! deserted him ! and cast him off
To bide the cold world's pity or its scoff !
Her letters, which were once so warm, grew cold,
And all that he could dread too plainly told ;
And rumours reached him that she smiled on one
Whose path was gilded by a brighter sun.

 Stung to the nerve—a wound too keen to bear—
He struggled not, but sank into despair ;

How deep his anguish was, ah ! who shall say ?
What dreams were his by night, what thoughts by day ?
Thus goaded on by agony, at last
He reached the brink of madness ! There, aghast
At the dread gulf he stood, and, ere too late,
Resolved to rise superior to his fate.
There was in Arthur's character a high
And manly principle which could not die ;
A strength of purpose not to be subdued
By all the shocks of life, however rude.
Although his looks might make a stranger think
His soul was one that soon would quail or shrink.
But, no ! the instant his resolve was made,
His faculties of mind at once obeyed.
He took and burnt her letters, all but *one*,
He could not bring himself to burn *that one*.
Fancy, which sees through all things unrestrained,
Can guess what precious words *that one* contained.
He banished from his breast the killing thought,
Flew to his books, and, in their study, sought
To triumph o'er despair ; he went down deep
In speculations, till benumbing sleep
Would call him to repose ; he climbed on high,
New lands of human knowledge to descry,
Until his sight grew dim ; and thus his mind
Expanded, and he learned to read mankind.
He left no hour unoccupied, but strove
To discipline his thoughts that fain would rove.
And when the engagements of the day were o'er,
He sometimes sought his friends as heretofore,
But not to talk, as once, of trivial things,
But teach his mind to use her new-found wings.
Thus did he struggle with affliction's storm—
Thus from his thoughts he banished Helen's form.

Yet no vindictive feelings soured his mind,
His generous bosom glowed for all mankind ;
He loved her still, no blame on her he cast,
He only wanted to forget the past—
Forget the blow which all his hopes destroyed—
Forget the dream of love he once enjoyed ;
For Arthur knew it is not wise or well
Too long on pleasures that are past to dwell.
   Time fled ; and tidings came that sent a chill
Along my veins. I heard my friend was ill.
It took me unprepared ; for he again
Had ceased to write, it would have given him pain,
And, living far asunder, not a word
Had reached my ear of all that had occurred.
   Again we met. How glad we were to meet—
The friendship of old friends is doubly sweet.
But Arthur's looks were changed ; his cheek was white,
And his sunk eye flashed forth a feverish light.
Consumption's long lean fingers had been laid
Upon him, and his frame her touch obeyed.
The high heroic effort of my friend
To bear the death-stroke of his hopes, and bend
His sad reflections from the onward course
In which they hurried with a torrent's force,
Had proved too much for him ; a quick decay
Of health succeeded, and his strength gave way.
He came back conqueror from the mental strife,
But victory's wreath seemed purchased with his life.
And yet his looks were cheerful as before ;
No signs of latent grief his countenance wore ;
His cheeks were radiant with their wonted smiles ;
His lips were instinct with their former wiles ;
And I was sanguine that my friend erelong
With change of scene would soon again be strong.

The sunshine of the soul which he enjoyed
Was proof against ill-health and hopes destroyed.
Arthur had long been striving to withdraw
From all earth's vain dependencies ; he saw
Their futile nature, and he sought and found
The only true and firm support ; he found
The power that cleaves a pathway through the wave—
The power that leads to victory o'er the grave !
Though ill in health—a prisoner to one spot—
The playmate of his youth was ne'er forgot.
The graceful little sketch, First Love, which he
Had drawn at my request, and sent to me,
It seems he thought unworthy of his skill ;
And therefore he resolved, though weak and ill,
To draw another, and, as was his plan
When once resolved, with promptitude began.
But, ah ! how weak he was he scarcely knew ;
Yet still from day to day, he drew and drew,
A little at a time, until, at length,
So greatly had disease impaired his strength,
He one day almost fainted as he sat
And wrought upon it ! So my friend with that
Gave up the attempt. The drawing I possess
Unfinished, but I prize it none the less.
My friend grew slowly worse ; the sight was sad
But yet instructive, for his soul was glad ;
Oft ere the sun of human life declines,
The moon of future joy distinctly shines !
It was his frequent and his fervent prayer
That patience might be given him to bear
His illness to its end ; from fear set free
Of either when or what that end might be ;
And ever anxious what was wrong to shun,
He piously would add, " Thy will be done ! "

Thus with a will subjected and resigned
He viewed the future with a tranquil mind ;
He feared not death—we know that come it must,
And Arthur felt a never-failing trust
That, come what would, all would with him be well:
And his was not the spirit to rebel.
His fervent faith was fixed on Him who gave
His precious life a guilty world to save.
　Faith may be likened to the powerful chain
Which holds the ship that dances on the main,
A bond invisible—like that of love—
Binding the spirit to the world above.
It is a holy confidence and trust
In that great sacrifice, in which the Just
Died for the unjust—He who secret dwelt
From all eternity, unseen, yet felt ;
Who forth from ancient darkness called the earth,
And clothed with dewy green its lordly girth ;
And hung the dome of heaven with censers bright,
And bade them burn with ever-living light.
Low in the dust Faith reverently bends,
Nor tries to solve what human thought transcends ;
Then, rising, looks with confidence on high,
And does Heaven's will without inquiring, " Why ? "
So when the world was wrapped in waters dark,
The lonely dove flew homeward to the ark ;
Its length, its breadth, its plan were not her care,
She only knew that there was safety there.
　Time slowly wore away.　Meanwhile, my friend
Grew gradually worse.　At length his end
Seemed to be come ; severe spasmodic pain
Such as his ebbing strength could scarce sustain,
The sufferer bore ; while every hour they thought
Would bring him that dismissal which he sought.

But e'en in death imaginative still
His breast one thought with pleasure seemed to fill :
The thought that if his life that day should end,
The first that he in Paradise would spend
Would be a Sabbath, and his soul seemed blest
In contemplation of that heavenly rest.
His pain, at length, subsided, and his mind
Was given to see for what it was designed ;
The words, " Thy will be done," with which
He closed each wish and prayer, were words which he
    supposed
Came from his heart, though by his lips expressed,
And found, he thought, an echo in his breast ;
But now he saw distinctly in his mind
How easier far it is for poor mankind
To *say,* " The will of Providence be done,"
Than to receive it ; and he felt like one
Whom tribulation had refined, and taught
The state in which to use them as he ought.
And Arthur wished that none, from day to day,
Might use them in a light or thoughtless way ;
But rather in that state obtain a part
In which they might adopt them from the heart.
    And now when Arthur's end seemed drawing nigh,
When all earth's shadowy scenes must fade and
    die,
One darling passion still survived, to cast
A halo round the present and the past.
Undying love ! triumphant o'er decay,
Still in his breast bore undiminished sway.
His Helen, dear in life, in death was dear,
And, though far off, her image still was near ;
On her he cast no blame : he thought her will
Was warped by others, and he loved her still.

On her he cast no blame : nor yet do I,
If she is happy—well.   I pass her by.
I said he burnt her letters—all but *one ;*
There was, it seems, a something in *that one*
At once so dear, so soothing to his heart,
He felt that with *that one* he could not part ;
But now, when death seemed near, his love inspired
An act which must for ever be admired ;
The inward struggle might perhaps be hard—
It shows the more his delicate regard.
Anxious at heart that nothing might remain
Of which the exposure might afford her pain,
Or prove her fickle, what did Arthur do ?
To shield her from reproach he burnt *that* too !
He had a ring inlaid with Helen's hair,
Which she, it seems, had given him to wear
In days departed, when his hopes were high,
And life was gilded by a cloudless sky :
This ring he now produced—gazed at it long—
Felt in his breast emotions deep and strong—
Called it his greatest treasure upon earth,
To show how highly he esteemed its worth—
And, while the memory rose of other years,
Over it wept ungovernable tears.
This precious ring he bade his sister take,
Requesting her to keep it for his sake.
    His life, he said, on taking a review,
Had been a happy one : he thought that few
Had been so happy.   Men at life may chide,
But Arthur gazed upon its sunniest side ;
The wind, he not unfrequently would say,
Had been, through mercy, tempered day by day
To the shorn lamb, and he believed still would :
His faith was firm that all was for his good.

From quite the first he thought that he should die,
And now, when that event seemed drawing nigh,
Little remained for him to do but wait
Calmly and cheerfully his wished-for fate.
The blessed hope, which nothing could destroy,
Of free salvation and of future joy   .
Through the Redeemer, whom he loved so well:
This was the theme on which he chose to dwell.
He longed to go away and be at rest
Among the happy, happy, happy blest—
To be where no temptation can allure—
To be where all is holy—all is pure.

One night when all the firmament was bright
With heaven's eternal chalices of light,
And the pale crescent's rays in silence fell
On roof, and village spire, and distant dell,
Slept on the cold and moss-encrusted tomb,
And pierced the curtains of the dim sick-room ;
Arthur, whose pious thoughts were wont to tend
From outward objects to his journey's end,
Said that, in years elapsed and times gone by,
He often had enjoyed the starry sky—
Enjoyed the dreamy hush, the calm profound
Of many a moonlight scene outspread around ;
But now, far higher joys—all bright—all pure—
Not fading joys, but joys that would endure,
He hoped to share, in that blest City, soon,
Which needeth not the light of sun or moon.

How does Consumption, with a slow decay,
Waste the stout frame and steal the strength away ;
Yet never fails to whisper in the ear,
False, flattering words, that cheat us while they cheer ;
The face acquires a spiritual cast—
Full of the future, heedless of the past ;

And while the cheek foregoes its roseate dye,
A livelier brightness flashes from the eye ;
Till worn-out nature fails, and then the breath
Grows faint and fainter till it stops in death.
So the poor land-bird, borne by tempests rude,
Far mid the sea's mysterious solitude,
Wings on her anxious way, in hopes to see
Erelong some verdant isle or leafy tree ;
But only finds unstable waves instead
Beneath her feet and far around her spread.
Weary and faint, she makes a plaintive cry—
Her heart beats quick ; she can no farther fly.
Life still is dear ! Once more she forward springs—
Her last attempt—and flaps her little wings,
Then droops, and droops, and droops ; strives still to keep
Her onward course, and sinks into the deep.
    Thus drooped from day to day my early friend,
Not hating life, nor fearful of his end ;
Around his lips benignant smiles still played,
While each kind act his gratitude repaid.
And well was Arthur nursed : one, ever nigh,
Foresaw his wishes with a sister's eye.
Blest be the sex to whom it doth pertain
To add to pleasure and to take from pain !
Once, as she watched him at the dead of night,
He woke with eyes all radiant with delight,
And said he was *so* happy ; he had had
Such a sweet dream ! his very soul seemed glad.
He said that, in a vision, he had been
Up into heaven, heard judgment passed, and seen
The mysteries of the spirits' dwelling-place ;
Seen angel forms ; seen all except the face
Of the Eternal ! And he seemed to burn
Again to go, and never more return.

He drooped, and drooped, and drooped, until, at last,
His weakened intellect became o'ercast
With dark delirious clouds; yet gleams of light
Would sometimes flash athwart his mental night,
And with a sweetly animated face,
In which hope, peace, and joy had each a place,
He faintly would ejaculate a prayer
To be released, and be admitted there
Where pain afflicts no more, no griefs molest,
The worn are soothed, the weary are at rest !
Even the wanderings of his mind disclosed
How much his heart on heavenly things reposed.
He seemed to think a chariot, by-and-by,
Would come in pomp and bear him to the sky !
Even to Him whom he was wont to call
His hope of glory and his all in all.
In tranquil stillness lay the dying saint ;
He showed no fear, he uttered no complaint,
And thus he fell into a peaceful sleep
And woke no more ! For in that peaceful sleep
The silver chord was broken, and away
His soul took wing to realms of endless day.
    The funeral morn arrived.   For Arthur's sake
I sought the scene, howe'er my heart might ache ;
The morn was cold, although the sun was bright,
Ten thousand dewdrops glittered in his light ;
Autumn's rich tints had beautifully dyed
The hedges and the woods on either side;
The birds flew merrily from spray to spray,
And Nature gloried in her own decay.
With heavy heart I joined the funeral train,—
The heart will grieve, tho' sorrow may be vain.
We reached the grave, and there with deep-felt awe
These eyes the last sad ceremony saw !

There lay my friend ! no more the purple rill
" Boiled through his veins," but all was cold and
    still.
No joy—no gentle voice—not e'en a breath !—
How silent is the dreary house of death !
It seemed too small, too cramped a dwelling-place
For one whose thoughts once ranged o'er time and
    space.
And, standing by his grave, I sorrowing cast
A long, long look on years forever past,
When we were wont to meet, and, grave or gay,
Walk forth together at the close of day.
Of one so dear how strange to feel bereft !
Why was my friend thus taken—or I left ?
My mind became bewildered and o'erwrought,
And feeling seemed to triumph over thought.
Some tears perhaps I shed—for I am weak,
But tears look strange on manhood's stubborn cheek.
    And when the train of mourners had withdrawn,
The people had dispersed, and all were gone,
Except a few small children on the green,
With eyes intent still gazing on the scene,
I saw a man, whom years had made to bend,
Heaping the earth o'er my lamented friend !
A man whose head was silvered o'er with age—
Old, yet without the wisdom of the sage—
A man whose thoughts perhaps had never pass'd
Beyond the sphere in which his lot was cast.
One whose dull mind no promise seemed to give,
Whom haply no one loved, or wished to live—
Heaping the earth o'er one in manhood's spring,
Whose mind had ever been upon the wing ;
Who had at once such wisdom and such worth,
So much of Heaven while yet upon the earth,—

Who gave such promise for a future day,—
Whom many loved so well!   I turned away.
     My narrative is done.   It is no tale ;
Truth over fiction must at last prevail.
With the sad strain my plaintive harp still rings,
And tones of sorrow vibrate on its strings.
It may be wrong to grieve—it may be vain,
And yet, sometimes, 'twere shocking to refrain.
I have lost much in Arthur.   He is gone
To pluck the immortal rose that has no thorn.
I know full well no tears my eyes need dim
For Arthur's sake, for all is well with him ;
Nor would I fetch him from his glorious sphere,
Once having died, again to sojourn here ;
But looking back on pleasures that are past,
How blank it seems to stand alone at last !
I look around, but none can take *his* place ;
I miss his kindred heart, his well-known face.
Obliging looks and pleasant smiles abound,
But kindred hearts are not so quickly found.
Oh, what a zest to life does friendship give !
Without its sweets, O ! who would wish to live ?
But ah ! our dearest friendships here below,
A thousand things conspire to overthrow.
They seem like bubbles on the waves uptost,
Which every moment may be burst and lost.
Not like those friendships in the world above
Where love is friendship, friendship, too, is love—
First Love is last love—nothing can divide—
Distance or death, misfortune, wind, or tide ;
No coldness—no caprice—no love of change—
No idle longings for a wider range,
But where life's pilgrims, all their wanderings o'er
Though parted once on earth, can part no more.

Twelfth Month 31*st*, 1834.—The waning year is almost gone! Though it has brought its share of sorrows and disappointments, I must acknowledge, with gratitude, that I am blest in many ways, and I greatly desire that I may not be an unworthy recipient of the bounty of an all-benevolent Providence.

CHAPTER VIII.

Poetical contribution rejected—"The Friendless Poet"—
"The Village Shopkeeper"—His mother's death—
Mechanics' Institute — Introduction to O'Connell —
"Sonnet" to O'Connell—Visit to Devon—"Sonnet" to
Jonathan Dymond—Return Home—Melancholy thoughts
—"Sonnet" thereon—"Ode on Mutability."

Third Month 3rd, 1835.—My birthday. The fourth
and fifth cantos of my poem "The Phantom Land"
having been rejected in the last two numbers of the
Monthly Magazine, my hopes of bringing myself into
notice as a poet seem now to be extinguished. Every
avenue of literary distinction seemed to be closed
against me, and with a heavy heart I submitted to
my lot. I had done all that I was able to do, but
had failed; and I could not reproach myself, on the
one hand, with inglorious indolence, or, on the other,
with want of honourable perseverance.

But I did not for one moment relinquish my attach-
ment to poetry, and I determined still to write though
I might never be read. Although I had failed in my
endeavours, I did not despair of ultimate, though
far off, success.

THE FRIENDLESS POET.

Neglected, poor, dispirited, unknown,
The friendless poet wears his life away;
The world to him appears a desert lone,
The sun shines darkling at the noon of day.

Alone he walks at eve the billowy shore,
  What time the moon gleams on the waste below.
And sings to the deep bass of ocean's roar,
  The story of his soul's melodious woe.

He sees a thousand silver-crested waves
  That seek, ambitiously, to scale the skies,
Thrusting each other to untimely graves,
  While other thousands on their ruins rise.

A crowd of stars adorn the vault of night;
  He marks them glittering with conflicting rays,
Such numbers strive to shine that each, though
    bright,
  Shines unobserved amid the general blaze.

So fares it in the Temple of Renown;
  A dazzling concourse crowds the ivory floor,
And, while their lustre shines each other down,
  They keep the friendless poet at the door.

Yet Hope, undying Hope! man's faithful friend,
  Heaven's darling gift, the mourner's secret stay,
Unfailing Hope keeps by him to the end,
  And lifts her torch to cheer his darksome way.

The following poem may be a characteristic description of many a country tradesman :—

THE VILLAGE SHOPKEEPER.

These many years I now have stood
Behind this counter of oak-wood;
And now, at length, I seem grown old,
And find I cannot bear the cold.

My counter is my real estate,
Which I have tilled early and late,
And, having reaped a middling crop,
'Tis time, methinks, to shut up shop.

These eyes are not what once they were,
I have to use another pair ;
My active limbs are now grown weak,
My voice pipes strangely when I speak,
My memory, too, begins to fail,
And something seems my feet to ail,
My head is getting bald at top,
Tis time, methinks, to shut up shop.

My name, inscribed above my door
Some forty years ago or more,
None now can read.   My threshold, too,
Is worn by many a worn-out shoe.
My goods, that line these shelves about,
Belong to fashions long gone out.
Fair trade hath lost its sterling prop,
'Tis time, methinks, to shut up shop.

Old customers, who every morn
Would come and chat, are dead and gone ;
Along the churchyard, as I pass,
I see their names above the grass.
My youngers, too, whom I have seen
Grow up from children on the green,
Into the grave I see them drop,
'Tis time, methinks, to shut up shop.

During the summer of this year, my father suffered
much from his old complaints—dizziness in the head

and attacks of faintness. He was afraid to be left alone, and unable to take much exercise. My mother, also, was out of health, owing to a cough which had long been undermining her strength. My brother and I of course felt much anxiety about them, in addition to our other sources of disquietude.

Tenth Month 7th.—My dear mother is ill, very ill; but so placid, so beautiful, so uncomplaining.

Eleventh Month 2nd.—My uncle, Bracy Clark, F.L.S., is come to see us. The principal object of his visit was to see my dear mother. Her complaint was pulmonary consumption; and though we were continually flattered with hopes of her recovery, as is usual in such cases, yet the insidious disease advanced with a rapid and steady pace, till her strength was so much reduced that she was unable to walk upstairs.

As my mother was unable to take much solid food on account of the soreness of her mouth, and had no daughter now to make custards and other delicacies for her, and our servant had plenty of other employment, I learned to make them myself. It was a satisfaction to me thus to be able to minister to the comfort of one who in years past had done so much for me.

It was on the morning of the 11th of Eleventh Month that my father hastily entered our room with the same agonised expression of countenance which I had seen him wear on two former occasions. He came to tell us that my mother was dying, and that we must come immediately. We were soon dressed, and at her bedside. She was breathing quickly, and evidently near her end; but she was quite sensible, though her articulation was almost gone.

All that she uttered with regard to the state of her mind on this solemn occasion were the words, "No condemnation." She gradually fell into a gentle slumber, or state of unconsciousness, and thus she peacefully expired.

Oh! what a blank I feel! How many tears have I shed! But this is one of the conditions of the tenure of life. May I, from this time forth, cultivate in an increased degree those virtues which my beloved mother possessed; that when I come to die there may be no cloud, no shadow, but the pure sunshine of eternal life!

Farewell, my beloved mother! I shall no more see thee in thy armchair by the fireside; or on the grass plat, underneath the mulberry tree, with thy little silver fork partaking of the delicious newfallen purple fruit of which thou wast so fond!

During my mother's illness I saw Halley's celebrated comet. It was near the Great Bear. In size it was about equal to the stars in that fine constellation, but less brilliant. The tail of the comet was an extremely faint line of light, extending about one degree, and then lost in indistinctness; something like the track of a common meteor, but not so vivid. I gazed upon this wonderful circumnavigator of the solar system, which has been the subject of so much fine speculation and profound mathematical labour, with an interest which I cannot express.

Eleventh Month 24th.—I attended a public meeting this afternoon on the subject of the proposed Eastern

Counties Railway. There are a great many thick-headed men who see strange fears, and declare that it will be an injury to the town, and so forth; but I hail the project as a most noble and advantageous adventure.

I, at length, concluded to become a member of the Mechanics' Institution; and when the next election of committee-men occurred I was chosen one of that body. For some time I took no part in the business of the Committee; but contented myself with being an observer. The Institution was by no means in a flourishing condition. At length I drew up a series of propositions, and laid them before the Committee. These propositions were:—First, for a considerable reduction in the charge for membership, in order to induce a much larger number to join the Institution; secondly, for the opening of a reading-room, to be well supplied with London and local newspapers, and literary journals, for the use and improvement of the members; and, thirdly, for the allowing of each member to bring a female friend with him to hear the lectures, in order to have larger audiences on such occasions.

These sweeping reforms in the constitution of the Mechanics' Institution were accordingly submitted to the members at the General Meeting, and as there was every probability that the Institute would fall to the ground unless some remedial measures were carried, there was but little opposition to them, and they were finally adopted. A new Committee was chosen to carry these reforms into operation, and I was appointed Honorary Secretary to the Institu-

tion. The result answered my most sanguine expec-
tations.

On the 27th of Fifth Month I met with an adventure. This was an interview which I obtained with
Daniel O'Connell, the great agitator, the Liberator of
Ireland, the most distinguished man of the age. A
neighbour of ours called upon us in the morning to say
that O'Connell was about to pass through Colchester,
and would stop at the Cups Hotel to breakfast. I
was just in time to be introduced, with others, by
David Morris to O'Connell, with whom, to my great
satisfaction, I had the honour of shaking hands.

O'Connell! thou has brought into the field
Millions of heroes panoplied to fight
For Ireland, their freedom, and their right;
Brave injured men determined not to yield.
How hast thou armed them ?   Not with weapons bright,
Not with the sword, with which barbarians fight.
Public opinion is the sword they wield,
It sheds no blood, yet puts whole hosts to flight;
And thou hast given them a seven-fold shield,
Through which the spear of war can never smite,
Passive resistance to oppressive might !
Thine are the triumphs of a peaceful field,
Therefore I honour thee, and place thy name
Amidst the permanent great heirs of fame.

On the 28th of Seventh Month, 1836, I took coach
in order to pay a visit to my friends in Devonshire.
One of them showed me about Exeter; and not the
least interesting visit which we paid was to the grave
of Jonathan Dymond, the great Christian moralist.

DYMOND'S GRAVE.

Standing by Exeter's cathedral tower
My thoughts went back to that small grassy mound
Which I had lately left—the grassy mound
Where Dymond sleeps. I felt how small the power
Of timeworn walls to waken thoughts profound
Compared with that green spot of sacred ground.
Dymond ! Death-stricken in thy manhood's flower,
Thy brow with deathless amaranth is crowned ;
Thou saw'st the world from thy sequestered bower
In old hereditary errors bound ;
And such a truthful trumpet thou didst sound
As shall ring in men's ears till time devour
The vestiges of nations. Yet thy name
Finds but the tribute of slow-gathered fame.

We made a delightful excursion along the coast to
Dawlish, Teignmouth, Babbacomb, and Torquay.
On the day following we walked to Dawlish, and
having loitered a long while among the rocks of that
beautiful coast, we took boat and enjoyed a most
delighful row to Exmouth, whence we walked to my
uncle Henry Clark's pleasant cottage at Withycombe.
But as to our various adventures in this journey, and
our sayings and doings by sea and land, it is sufficient, perhaps, that they should be inscribed alone
on the pleasant pages of memory. I bade farewell
to my kinds friends on the 20th of the Eighth Month,
and embarked on board a steamboat at Exmouth for
London. After a voyage of 320 miles I arrived at
London about noon on the 22nd, immediately mounted a coach, and reached home the same evening.

After my return, and when the excitement of the journey was over, I began deeply to feel my forlorn condition. The future was impenetrably dark—the torch of Hope burnt dimly—and I could not see the steps of my feet. Frequent and earnest were my prayers to the Giver of every good and perfect gift that He would grant me His blessing and shed a light upon my path.

SONNET.

Oh! for a mind congenial with my own!
Loving whatever is divine in thought,
And beautiful in vision. Life is short,
My youth is past, and I am still alone.
Oh! for a friend with kindred feelings fraught
To love me, cheer me, and, with skill untaught,
Forth from my heart-strings call each slumbering tone;
One of the true imaginative sort
To whom I might, confidingly, make known
What glorious pageants sometimes sweep athwart
My visual range, and vanish into nought,
Whither the poet's bubble worlds are blown.
Is there a voice that can respond to mine?
Or must my life in loneliness decline?

Tenth Month 10*th.*—Finished my ode on " Mutability," the first of my series of Sacred Odes.

ODE ON MUTABILITY.

The dead, the dead, the mighty dead!
How silent are they in their mouldy graves.
The dead, the dead, the mighty dead,
Over them all her wand Oblivion waves.

The dead, the mighty dead ;
Great men of great observance in their day,
  How is their greatness fled !
How is their glory blown, like smoke, away !
Into what degradation are they cast !
Into what ill condition are they come !
Statesmen, whose eloquence held nations fast,
  How soon their lips are dumb !
Monarchs, who ruled the empires of the past,
How small the realms o'er which they rule at last !
The dead, the dead, the mighty dead,
Neither the stirring tumult of the drum,
  Nor yet the trumpet's blast,
Nor yet the excitement of resounding arms,
  Nor Glory's mead, nor beauty's charms,
Nor pomp, which is the allurement of the vain,
Nor praise, which is the guerdon of the great,
Nor boundless power, nor still more boundless gain,
Nor fear, nor jealousy, nor love, nor hate,
Nor any might that magic may possess,
  Can win them back from nothingness,
    And bid them breathe again.

Cast thine eye Eastward.   Dost thou now behold
Yon plain outspread in sterile disarray,
Through which yon sleepy stream winds its dull way ?
There Babel's city towered in years of old,
The rich the great, the beautiful, the gay,
Where is she now ? remingled with earth's mould.
O'er all her pomp the tide of time has rolled
And left her to the scorching winds a prey.
Her walls, her baths, luxuriously cold,
Her gorgeous domes, that glittered in the day,
Her hanging gardens sweet as sweet Cathay,

Her princes proud, her chiefs and captains bold,
Who quaffed potations from their cups of gold,
With all her sons born only to obey,
Each with his little history untold,
All are demolished in one vast decay!
And Bel is tumbled from his lofty keep,
And what was once his temple is a heap,
   A blasted heap!
 A place untenanted by men,
A cage for unclean birds, a lion's den,
A wrath-struck object of offended might,
 A mark for thunderbolts to smite.

   The living, too, are hastening fast
    Away, away,
   To join the pilgrims of the past
    In their decay.
   Beauty, in all its bloom,
   Goes down into the tomb
    An early prey.
   The dearest, brightest, best,
    How short their stay!
   Treasures which, ere possessed,
    Are snatched away.
   The old man bent with time,
   The strong man in his prime,
    The young, the gay,
   All take the same sad road,
   All seek their long abode,
    All pass away.
The path of years is as the mournful scene,
Of some great army's flight,
Where all the way tells tales of what has been,
Strewed as it is with wrecks of former might,

Chariots o'erthrown, and trophies cast aside,
Ensigns and arms, and spoils of human pride.

But not on man alone
Is seen the hand of change ;
From the Antarctic to the Arctic zone
All Nature, through her vast and varied range,
Feels the mutations of progressive Time,
Along his track sublime.
Old shores are sinking down into the deep,
New isles are springing from the foamy wave,
Winds to the earth the oaks of ages sweep,
earthquakes whelm whole cities in one
grave,
Rivers that were—are not—
Or, fallen into infancy again,
Run prattling to the main.
The very rocks enjoy no sacred lot ;
Mere dropping water eats into their grain ;
Vexed between moist and dry, and cold and hot,
Nature, Earth's mother, never ends her toils—
What Summer ripens, Winter quickly spoils.
But yesterday a bud—a flower to-day—
To-morrow nothing—such is Nature's way !
'Tis all a drama on the world's great stage,
Wherein each day, with all its joys and woes,
Its little triumphs, and its petty rage,
Is but a shifting scene which quickly goes ;
And night lets down the curtain at the close.
Thus scene succeeds to scene,
While wakeful birds sing symphonies between.
The rising sun reveals another morn,
But yesterday is gone !

The stars alone, that walk the solemn sky,
Or stand bright sentinels at Heaven's gate,
Seem of a race created not to die ;
Their golden shields nightly attract the eye,
Gleaming afar beyond the reach of fate ;
The emblems of eternity they shine,
Age after age with unimpoverished light,
Over the pure transparent hyaline
Gently, untarnishably, softly bright,
Orion and Arcturus in their might,
The same that Job saw in old times and lands,
     When God, who doeth all things right,
     Left him to Satan's hands ;
The same the shepherds of Chaldee of yore
Regarded as they roamed their mountains o'er,
     Watching their flocks by night ;
And which the weary-hearted of all times,
After the tumult of the passing day,
With all its aching cares and all its crimes,
Have looked upon, and could not turn away—
So touched, so moved, while all the host above
Looked down on them with undissembled love,
And bade their calmèd spirits to rejoice
With their resistless inarticulate voice.

And yet that host, though clothed with Heaven's light,
When Time's dread dial marks the appointed hour,
Shall, on a sudden, trembling with affright,
Feel the invisible strong arm of power ;
And like a routed army take to flight ;
Their golden shields—the glory of all eyes—
Like those that Solomon in Salem wrought,
Of which the Egyptian warrior made proud prize,
     Shall benefit them nought.

Stars against stars in wild dismay shall run,
    And vanish one by one.
And fear the inhabitants of earth shall stun ;
Fierce winds shall whip the sea's affrighted flood ;
The undulating moon shall roll in blood,
    And darkness dim the sun.
And there shall be on high a fearful sound,
And Night shall spread her manifold curtain round,
Lit only by the lightning's blinding flash ;
    And, 'mid the general crash,
The universe, dissolving, shall take fire ;—
Earthquakes shall agonise the bursting globe ;—
The skies shall rend asunder as a robe ;—
The elements shall melt with fervent heat ;— .
The rocks flow down ; the sea's proud waves retreat,
    And Nature shall expire.

And such is the inevitable fate
Which, like a sword suspended by a thread,
    Hangs over Nature's head ;
    And such the date,
Such is the short, uncertain, date of man,
Placed in this dim probationary state.
    O ! while we can,
    Ere yet it be too late,
Whither for sure protection shall we flee ?
Whither, O ! God, our Father, but to Thee ?
    Thy throne is sure,
Amidst the flood of ages without end,
    And still will be
When sun and moon no longer shall endure.
Thou only hast the shield that can defend ;
    And if with pure

And deep humility of heart we trust,
O God ! in Thy Almightiness to save,
It will not trouble us that we are dust,
And that our life is bounded by the grave ;
For Thou canst soothe us at our latest breath,
   And give an angel's smile to death.
Yes ! Thou canst make our last our happiest day,
And in the boundless riches of Thy love,
Canst give us an inheritance above
   That fadeth not away.

I have now reached that point of time in my life at which I commenced this narrative. Very far from having arrived at that state of perfectness which is obtainable through Divine assistance in this state of being, I may confess that, from my childhood, I have lived in the practice of daily and still more frequent prayer. Not formal tedious oblations, but the short and fervent breathings of the heart. This practice has been of great use to me, and contributed to make me place a just value on temporal and eternal things, so that I have been at all times willing rather to sink unknown and unnoticed to the grave, than forfeit one single hope of a happy immortality.

We will now continue the narrative with extracts from his note books and other sources.

CHAPTER IX.

Death of his only brother—Delegate to the Anti-Corn Law Conference — Triumph of Free Trade — "Sonnet" thereon—Death of Sarah J. Grubb—" A Friends' Meeting in the Country."

Second Month 2nd, 1838.—Since I last made an entry in this book great and unlooked-for and melancholy events have taken place in our little family. On the 22nd of the Eleventh Month my dear and only brother, William Clark Hurnard, was taken in a fit. It was supposed to be occasioned by a fall from a gig some weeks before. Other fits followed. What anguish—what anxiety were ours! On the 5th of the First Month he died, between one and two in the morning.

He was buried on the 10th; thus am I left the last of the flock. I am not yet thirty, yet I have lived to see my two sisters and my only brother, after having grown up to maturity, summoned to another and a better world! How wonderful is this! For what purpose am I left? How long shall I remain behind? How desolate I am! Do Thou, O Lord, be pleased to bless me, and preserve me, and direct my steps, and enlighten my mind, and grant me Thy salvation!

Second Month 7th, 1842.—Went to London to attend the great Anti-Corn Law Conference as a deputy from

K

the Colchester Association. The meetings lasted
five days. The principal speakers were O'Connell,
George Thompson, Joseph Hume, Cobden, Villiers,
Joseph Sturge, Grey, Sharman Crawford, Dr. Bow-
ring, Taylor, Colonel Thompson, and Diogenes
Falvey, a working man. The meetings were highly
interesting; and I feel assured, from the spirit which
was exhibited, that the Corn Laws will soon be
swept away.

Having spent about five years of my youth in the
United States as one of a family of emigrants subjected to many hardships, and deprived of much of
the school education which I should otherwise have
received, but, at the same time, learning many prac-
tical lessons from experience, and observation of men
and things, I naturally imbibed many opinions which
have greatly influenced my subsequent life.

One of the most striking facts which arrested my
notice was the prodigal abundance of food which the
people enjoyed.

The interminable market place of Philadelphia,
stretching throughout the city, glutted with every
kind of country produce, and lengthening as the city
extended, was a sight never to be forgotten.

The quantity of food which was habitually wasted
at table would have amply fed an English family.
Not only bread, the staff of life, but fish, flesh, fowl,
and fruit abounded in marvellous profusion. On the
return, therefore, of my family to our native land,
when I was sixteen years of age, I was shocked to
witness the poverty of the working classes, and the
struggle of the trading community to obtain a living,

overburdened as they were with taxes, the result of useless wars and restrictive laws.

The Corn Laws especially, which prevented the importation of foreign grain except when home-grown corn reached a famine price, filled me with disgust. These laws were plainly designed by a landlord-Parliament to raise the rent of land by diminishing the supply of food to the people. The interference with the principles of Free Trade sometimes produced commercial panics and great distress throughout the country; sometimes even a sanguinary civil war seemed to threaten the land. At length the Anti-Corn Law League was established at Manchester, the object of which was to overthrow the existing monopoly under which the country groaned, and thereby encourage the free exchange of home manufactures for foreign corn. The leaders of this wonderful organisation were Richard Cobden and John Bright, whose enormous exertions, sagacious tactics, and convincing eloquence, triumphed after a seven years' crusade. The principles which they advocated were sound and true ; and, although the hostility which they encountered was powerful and bitter beyond what the present generation can conceive, yet at last they convinced and subdued their adversaries. Sir Robert Peel, who was raised to the post of Prime Minister in order to maintain the Corn Laws, and the new Parliament which he summoned to support him, proved, ultimately, to be the very Minister, and the very Parliament, which abolished these iniquitous laws.

The common manufactures and commerce of the

country have been enormously increased by Free
Trade ; and the prosperity and happiness of the
people consequently enhanced.

I look back on no labours of my life with more
satisfaction than the zealous efforts which I made to
promote the success of the Anti-Corn Law League,
which, however, at the time, cost me the ill-will of
the influential people in my neighbourhood.

Fourth Month, 21st.—We have received four bales
of Anti-Corn Law packets, which I am to distribute
to the electors of this town. I find the League have
done me the honour to print my sonnet among the
selected contents of their packets, in company with
passages from Byron, Cowper, Elliot and others.

SONNET.

Why should our poor be exiled from the land
Of their progenitors, and forced to go
And seek a home in realms of ice and snow,
Enduring every hardship which the hand,
The heavy hand, of want can lay on woe,
And for no fault of theirs ?   'Twere better planned
To bring food home to them.   It is a grand
Mistake to fancy that we overflow
With population.   Men can never stand
Too thickly on the soil of England.   No !
Numbers give strength ; and if the winds might blow
Food to our harbours London might expand
On every side, until she reached the shore,
And John O'Groat beheld her at his door.

" It will be recollected," says the *Ipswich Express*

of July 11th, 1843, "that, during a recent debate on the Corn Laws in the House of Commons, Sir John Tyrrell, Bart., M.P. for North Essex, defied Richard Cobden, Esq., M.P. for Stockport, and leader of the Anti-Corn Law League, to meet him face to face before the farmers of Essex. Mr. Cobden accepted the challenge, and declared his readiness to discuss the principles of Free Trade and the principles of Protection, in the very division of the county which Sir John Tyrrell represents in Parliament. From the time that Mr. Cobden's intention was known, strenuous efforts were made to excite the farmers against that gentleman, and, by organisation, to ensure a signal defeat to the Free Trade party. The language employed by the local papers was of so angry a nature that some were not without apprehensions that Mr. Cobden would meet with personal violence."

Seventh Month 8th, 1843.—The day of the great Anti-Corn Law meeting at Colchester. Cobden obtained a complete victory over Sir John Tyrrell and his party. We had Cobden, Villiers, Diogenes, R. R. Moore, Harbottle, and several others to dinner, and, after the meeting, to tea with us. They were all in the highest spirits at the result.

Twelfth Month 5th, 1845.—Last night I read in the *Times* newspaper the joyful tidings that the Peel-Wellington Government has, at length, resolved to bring forward a measure for the total and immediate repeal of the Corn Laws at the commencement of the next session. The power of the League and the terror of approaching famine, with all its concomitant

evils, have combined to overthrow this oppressive
law, in spite of the most powerful aristocracy in the
world. Those who have laboured in the great work,
who have endured insult, contempt, ridicule, and
oppression for its sake, have a right to exult at the
victory, which will bring comfort and plenty to tens
of thousands of fire-sides in Great Britain, and will
be a blessing to Europe and America, and every other
country on the face of the globe.

. *Fifth Month* 16*th*, 1846.—Last night the Bill for the
repeal of the Corn Laws was read the third time in
the House of Commons, and passed by a majority of
ninety-eight.

Sixth Month 26*th*.—This day the Bill for the aboli-
tion of the Corn Laws received the Queen's assent.
Free trade for ever !

We have anticipated the course of events in
order to bring the account of the Anti-Corn Law
agitation to a conclusion, and now revert to an earlier
date.

Third Month 16*th*, 1842.—Died at Sudbury, Sarah
John Grubb, a distinguished female minister in our
Society. When young and unmarried she devoted
herself a good deal to open-air preaching in mar-
ket-places and elsewhere with great earnestness
and power.. During the latter part of her life
she lived in my own neighbourhood, and I knew
her well.

She was a woman of great natural gifts, and

possessed a depth of spiritual knowledge and a force
of polished language that were very remarkable. To
listen to her sometimes one seemed to be borne
upward calmly and steadily, as on eagle's wings, into
the very atmosphere and precincts of Heaven.

The following poem, descriptive of a Friends'
meeting in the country, gave me the opportunity of
describing, not only this remarkable female preacher,
but the several members of my own family, besides
some other characters familiar to me :—

A FRIENDS' MEETING IN THE COUNTRY.

A simple porch—an ancient pile,
Of no especial mark or style—
Green graves, and slumbering trees without—
Bare walls within, and timbers stout—
Here, at this evening hour, a band
   Of silent worshippers have met,
Female and male on either hand ;
   A narrow aisle between them set.
It is, indeed, a little band—
Long forms without a tenant stand,
And seats that ancient valiants bore—
Departed—know them now no more !
Yet over all a stillness dwells
   Than empty silence far more deep,
In which the heart with fervour swells,
   And fear and hope together weep.
But all are not alike engaged
   To bow their souls in praise or prayer :
The thoughts of some, like birds uncaged,
   Are wandering here or wandering there,

Unmindful of life's narrow span,
  Forgetful of the debt they owe
For every breath since life began,
  And every good enjoyed below!

What contrasts, both of mind and face,
Of youth and age are in this place!
What different thoughts and feelings stir
The brain of him—the heart of her!
That tender mother's fervent look
Is winning as an open book:
Her features are of Roman form,
Unmarked by passion's sun or storm;
Her face, indeed, is saintly fair—
Dark are her eyes; her silvery hair,
Worn short beneath her muslin cap,
  Peeps forth in little natural waves;
Her hands are folded in her lap;
  She is not one of fashion's slaves;
Alike her countenance and dress
Her loyalty to Heaven express.

This upright man, of sanguine hue,
  And stern, yet sorrow-stricken face,
Appears like one still struggling through
  The briars and thorns that mar life's race.
But though his head is crisped with gray,
  And though his brow is graved with care,
Hope lights his features with her ray,
  And faith defends him from despair.
Fighting in faith the fight of life,
Through grace he triumphs in the strife.

A girl is sitting by the wall,
Still young, but as a woman tall;

With face as dark, if not so sad,
As, haply, Jephthah's daughter had.
How still she sits in soul retired,
With peaceful thoughts of Heaven inspired.
Her eyes are wedded to the ground,
Moveless to either sight or sound.
Beside her sits a smaller girl
Complexioned like the ocean pearl;
The same in tippet and in frock—
In mind how different seems the stock
The ardent face, the fitful start
Reveal the young enthusiast's heart.

This stripling here with forehead high,
With pallid cheek and serious eye—
So fair a morn gives promise soon
To usher in a glorious noon.
Next him there sits a pretty boy
    Perhaps of ten years old or less,
To gaze upon him is a joy,
    Though quaint and homely is his dress.
The rose's blush is on his check,
    The diamond's light is in his eye,
His lips, though silent, seem to speak,
    His curly locks around him fly.
To sit in stillness is, to him,
An irksome task to every limb;
And so, the moments to beguile
    He calls his fancy to his aid,
With Xury sails full many a mile—
    With Crusoe wanders, half afraid;
Sees in the wainscot's knotted boards,
Exploding ships, and flaming swords;

The slough that Christian struggled thro'—
   The lions crouching in their lair—
Apollyon, terrible to view,
   The Doubting Castle of Despair !

Here sits a man whose heavy face
Of thought or feeling shows no trace ;
A man of long-descended wealth,
And richer still in changeless health ;
Respected in his daily walk,
But fitted for no higher talk
Than that of bullocks—or of crops—
Or how the glass creeps up—or drops ;
Contented in his rural sphere,
To one indulgent bosom dear.

Yon row of maidens young and fair
Have surely known no mother's care ;
In various colours sprucely dight,
   With bonnets gay, and tresses curled,
They seem just fledged to take their flight
   Into the giddy outside world.

Yon female Friend in middle life,
Though handsome, is not yet a wife ;
Though love in her benignant eyes
In gushing fountains seems to rise.
Unsullied as the silk she wears
Her soul a sacred impress bears.
She never loved—because unsought !
Or love too rashly set at nought !
Or if she loved 'twas unrevealed ;
And thrown away because concealed !

And so her warm affections find
Solace in helping all mankind—
The poor at home—the slave abroad
All who can yield her no reward!

On the raised benches, at the end,
Facing the meeting sits a Friend
Of reverend age. His visage meek
Seems a glad spirit to bespeak.
Goodness, untinged by worldly guile
Has framed his features to a smile.
A female preacher by his side
Sedately sits. Her forehead wide,
And short round features, full of lines,
Show, by indubitable signs,
Her mental energy and power,
Fitted for any place or hour.
She rises. In her form and mien
A natural dignity is seen.
Her Quaker bonnet, backward thrust,
Reveals her massive face ; her bust
Swells with her mission ; slow she speaks,
Her lifted hand due audience seeks :

" When Christ on earth in person came,
    He promised that where two or three
Are met together in His name—
    Which is His power—there He will be !
This day this promise we behold
Fulfilled amongst us. O'er Christ's fold
The hovering wing, it may be said,
Of ancient goodness still is spread !
God is a Spirit ! Boundless space
Is His eternal dwelling-place !

The earth is with His presence filled,
  Yet such is His mysterious plan,
His sacred pleasure is to build
  His temple in the heart of man!
And there in spirit to be sought,
  In spirit worshipped and obeyed,
Until salvation shall be wrought,
  And man is in His image made!
Nor is it strange that He who wheeled
  These worlds into the empty sky,
Yet paints the lilies of the field,
  And feeds the ravens when they cry,
Should condescend His works to own;
  And this the chiefest of the whole;
And cause His presence to be known
  In man's immortal quicken'd soul!

"This revelation from above
Within us shows the Father's love
To fallen man.   It is a lamp
To every soldier in His camp;
It is the hidden manna given,
From day to day, direct from heaven;
Yet daily to be sought—a brook
As by the way—a shepherd's crook,
To draw us to Himself—a well,
Pure, sweet, and inexhaustible,
Of living waters.   O, how great
The privilege!   How good the gift!
How excellent the Giver!   Wait
    In faith before Him.   He will lift
Our heads in hope.   We shall rejoice
    As in His presence, without fear;
Shall listen to His gracious voice,
    And feel in truth that God is near.

In this communion we shall know
  No need of outward form or sign
Or ceremonial, pomp, or show,
  Or sacramental bread and wine.
The blessed substance being ours
  These empty forms are worthless dross,
They yield to Christ's superior powers
  Who, dying, nailed them to His cross !

"What is true worship ?   Let each one
Ask his own heart.   Is it to run
With eager crowds, on words to feed ?
Is it to hear a parson read ?
Is it dependence on a priest ?
Is it to bow towards the east ?
Is it to listen to the sound
Of solemn music swelling round ?
True worship is a work divine,
  Wrought in the secret of the heart,
In which both God and man combine ;
  But man performs the minor part.
The soul with God brought face to face,
  Bows low before the King of kings,
Adores the wonders of His grace,
  And tribute to His footstool brings.
The power for which proud man aspires,
  The treasure prized above all price,
The will, the passions, the desires,
  Are offered up in sacrifice.
And God is pleased, in boundless love,
  To make His glorious presence felt,
Grant holy oneness from above,
  And all the soul in sweetness melt.

And God is gracious to the meek
   And low of heart who own His sway,
Who unto Him in spirit seek
   Through Jesus Christ the living Way.
This worship we may all perform,
   Each in our own peculiar sphere,
Amidst the ragings of the storm,
   When evil men are struck with fear;
Or in the calm of daily life,
   Whatever cares engage our hands,
Amidst the town's commercial strife,
   Or by the ocean's changing sands,
Though o'er the sea we steer our course,
   Or walk as in the cloudy night,
The soul may gather to the Source
   Of life divine, of love and light.

"Jesus is our High Priest.   His word
Within the waiting soul is heard,
Teaching as no man .ever taught.
The power to teach cannot be bought ;
It is the gift of God.   In vain
Men seek by study to attain
To heavenly knowledge.   Learning fails
To pluck from human eyes the scales
That blind men to the truth.   No doubt
   This people was raised up of old
To make resistance, meek yet stout,
   To human priestcraft, and uphold
A purer standard to mankind
   Of life and doctrine,—God's free grace,
And man's free will !   But they were fined,
   And mocked, and scourged from place to place;

Robbed by informers, rudely thrown
  Into foul dungeons, suffering through
Long months and years ; not men alone,
  But, likewise, tender women, too !
Yet could they glory in their wrongs,
  Nor hope nor confidence would yield ;
But raised to Heaven triumphant songs,
  And with their lives their witness sealed.
Oh, that in this more peaceful day,
  Those times by none may be forgot ;
Why should we cast our shield away,
  As though with oil anointed not ?
May neither pride nor sloth deter
  The heavenward progress of our youth.
Sell not your birthright ! Nor prefer
  A mess of pottage to the truth !

" Thanks be to God, who would that all
Should turn to Him and live. The call
Is universal. He hath done
His part in that He gave His Son
To die for sinners ; and hath placed
His Spirit in our hearts. Then haste
To seek this inward light. Obey
Its guidance in the heavenly way.
It leads unto the truth. It shows
  The vanity of earthly things ;
Reveals to man his inward foes,
  Perhaps unknown before ; and brings
His soul from bondage. It destroys
  All false, deceitful colours ; rends
The specious veil from worldly joys,
  And shows in what earth's glory ends !

This blessed light of truth disowns
   All fraud, all violence, all wars,
. All tyrannies of states or thrones,
   All harsh, unjust, oppressive laws !
It yields alone true peace of mind,
   It governs every vain desire,
Leads to truth-speaking with mankind,
   Plainness of language and attire ;
Brings into unity and love,
   That bond of love which nought can break ;
Binds us at once to Christ above.
   And to each other for His sake.
It is the diadem and crown
   Of our assemblies when we meet,
When all within us is laid down
   In nothingness at Jesus' feet !
It is the Unction from on high—
   The true Anointing, which alone
Can rightly fit and qualify
   To make the glorious Gospel known !
To this, dear friends, in love unfeigned,
   I now commend you, one and all,
With mine own soul ; I feel constrained
   Thus to invite you !   Heed the call ! "

She ceases.   She resumes her seat ;
Yet still would seem the cadence sweet
To melt upon the ear.   Around
A silence settles—calm, profound.
A glow of heavenly love arrays
Her face ; —but soon she kneels—she prays.

" O Thou ! whose dwelling is on high,
Look down upon us with an eye

Of love and mercy; and preserve
A remnant which shall never swerve
From Thy true service; but uphold
Thy standard in the earth, with bold
And faithful hearts! Shed forth Thy light,
And vindicate, in all men's sight,
Thy blessed truth! And, for the sake
Of Christ, our risen Lord, O take
Unto Thyself Thy mighty power!
Let not the sword of men devour
For ever; but be pleased to draw
The hearts of men away from war,
To worship Thee! O God! subdue
Our stubborn wills! Do Thou renew
Our spiritual strength. Forgive
Our erring hearts and bid us live!
Be Thou our Guide from day to day!
Thy law, O Lord, within us write!
Be Thou our hope, our help, our stay,
Who art the Truth—the Life—the Light—
That we may know a second birth;
For all men must be born again
Who seek to be redeemed from earth;
The second death will then obtain
No power to harm us. Cause, O Lord,
Thy truth to prosper more and more
In every land—at home, abroad—
That men Thy goodness may adore!
That holiness may yet increase,
And spread through earth from sea to sea,
And men may live in love and peace,
And welcome incense rise to Thee!
To Thee, O Father! and Thy Son,
The First Begotten from the dead,

L

And to the Holy Spirit—one
   True God ! our ever-living Head !
High praises be ascribed, both now
   And through eternity ; for Thou
   Art worthy ! "

The sunset's soft and yellow beam
Along the wall begins to gleam ;
The sparrows on the fir-trees nigh
Have ceased to chirrup.   By and by
The little company depart,
Some tendered and refreshed in heart ;
With every feature that they wear
Clothed in the garment of her prayer;
And grateful incense breathes above,
Accepted by celestial Love.

CHAPTER X.

Prize poem on Slavery : " Crowning Crime of Christendom "—
Commencement of friendship with Benjamin B. Wiffen—
" Master and Slave "—Sonnet " to a Blackbird "—" Ode
on the Death of Thomas Clarkson."

IN the year 1845, a gentleman of Bristol, of the
name of Edward Thomas, wishing to stimulate popular
hatred of slavery, offered a prize of £10 for the best
poem descriptive of a picture by Biard, which had
been exhibited at the Royal Academy, in 1840. It
represented a scene on the coast of Africa, in which
white men were buying negroes, both male and female,
from the native slave-traders, and branding them
with a hot iron, while a ship lay in the offing, ready
to convey them to a Christian land, across the ocean,
to toil, and suffer, and die in horrible slavery.

Not having seen the picture, I determined to write
a poem descriptive, not of it, but of the slave trade
as usually carried on.

Charles Gilpin, one of the judges, wrote to me to
inform me that Edward Thomas, the gentleman who
offered the prize of £10, had resolved to give two
prizes of that amount ; and also two second-class
prizes, consisting of copies of a large engraving of
Biard's picture ; and that one of these engravings
was allotted to me.

The following is the poem alluded to, which was

published in the *Anti-Slavery Reporter*, Fourth Month
1st, 1846 :—

THE CROWNING CRIME OF CHRISTENDOM.

> I saw in the visions of night,
>   An African village on fire !
> The flames rolled along in their might ;
> And the shrieks of the victims rose higher and higher,
> As of infant, and parent, and grey-headed sire.
>
> The man-stealers sprang on their prey !
>   And hundreds were slain or subdued :
> Some perished from utter dismay,
> And others were slain while for mercy they sued ;
> And the soil they had tilled with their blood was imbued.
>
> One sight I shall never forget,
>   Till the sunbeam of life is denied,
> And the star of my memory shall set—
> A bridegroom, self-slaughtered, enclasping his bride,
> Who lay murdered, and mangled, and scorched by his
>   side !
>
> The captives in fetters were bound ;
>   Fear ran through their tremulous frames ;
> And they sobbed as they gazed round and round,
> For where children that day had been playing their
>   games,
> There were carcasses, captives, and smouldering flames.
>
> The vision fled slowly away,
>   And another appeared in its place :—
> I looked on a beautiful bay ;
> And ships in tranquillity slept on its face :
> They were slavers ! the pest of the African race.

On the shore was a horrible mart
Where man was the merchandise sold ;
Where the best blood that boils through the heart
Was bartered, as though it were stolid and cold
As the storm-beaten rock or the slave dealer's gold.

Sweet babes from their mothers were torn—
Wives were rent from their husbands away—
Fond brothers asunder were borne—
And lovers were parted and sold far astray,
To clasp hands never more till the great judgment-day.

I heard them in anguish complain ;
For life without love is but dross !
But they pleaded for mercy in vain ;
For the demons, who swore by the creed of the Cross,
Turned their faces away with an insolent toss.

I gazed on the hot iron brand,
As it hissed on each ebony skin ;
I saw the slaves borne from the land
To a slave-ship, and packed in a large, loathsome bin,
Where the stench seemed to quench the dull light that
  stole in.

The vision fled slowly away,
And another appeared in its place :—
Far around flashed the bright ocean spray,
And a ship sped along in her beauty and grace,   [pace.
Bounding o'er the wild waves with the swift swallow's

But pestilence, madness, and death,
Raged and raved in her dark, crowded hold ;
And the slaves, as they drew their last breath,
Uncoffined, unwept, ere their limbs were yet cold,
O'er the tall vessel's side were remorselessly rolled !

Swift, swift, o'er the billowy main,
 Flew onward that death-stricken barque ;
And, following as swift, in her train,
Swam many a monstrous and ravenous shark,
Gorging freely their fill of the carcasses dark.

As I gazed the great deep was unsealed !
 I looked down on the broad ocean's bed ;
And a valley of bones was revealed,
Which shall yet be an army with banners outspread,
When the last trumpet sounds which shall waken the dead.

The vision fled slowly away,
 And another appeared in its place :—
Before me a fair region lay,
Where mountains rose high, like a huge giant race,
With sweet, flowery fields lying calm at their base.

That land was the land of the slave !
 The scene of his closing career ;
Where the generous, the fond, and the brave,
Toiled on in their manacles year after year,
Paid with stripes for their labour—their solace a jeer.

I saw them worn out with their toil,
 Urged on by the slave-driver's whip ;
I saw the lash cruelly coil   [drip
Round their scar-covered backs till the warm blood would
While a groan faintly fell from the eloquent lip !

Enslaved both in body and mind,
 The victims of grief and despair,
They seemed to their fortune resigned,
With no will of their own—for the future no care,
Like the dumb beasts of burden whose lot is to bear.

I beheld a poor African chief,
Whose name was once honoured afar ;
Yet meekly he bore with his grief,
And sang to himself, " Callabar ! Callabar !
Me could die in sweet peace could me see Callabar ! "

The vision fled slowly away,
And another appeared in its place :—
I witnessed the great judgment-day !
And the branded, down-trodden, enslaved negro race
With their tyrants and taskmasters stood face to face !

Then spake One from the cloud which He trod,
" *If man has no mercy on man,*
How can man hope for mercy from God ? "
And a cry of despair through the multitude ran,
" *There is no hope for men who have trafficked in man.*"

I have received a letter from Benjamin B. Wiffen,
who has seen my poem, and extols it in the highest
manner. This is most generous treatment in a perfect stranger of his standing, and I appreciate the
honour accordingly.

This was the commencement of a friendship which
lasted until the close of Benjamin B. Wiffen's life.

MASTER AND SLAVE.

Has this chained negro an immortal soul
Equal in God's impartial eye to thine ?
Doubtless ; then wherefore thus his limbs confine ?
Why scourge him till to Heaven his eye-balls roll,
Hopeless of human mercy ?   Slave though he be
He is thy brother Abel.   Love divine
The spirit of his inner man makes free ;

And on the altar of his poverty
A holy offering—pure—evangeline—
Sends up rich clouds of incense, such as He
Will have respect to who the heart can see,
Whose nostrils will be turned away from thine.
Prosper thou mayest, yet still it will be found,
In every age the murderer has found
The blood of Abel crieth from the ground.

TO A BLACKBIRD.

Sing, bonny blackbird! thy melodious lay
Proves that thy breast some heavenly spark contains:
Love, joy, and pride distend thy little veins
   As they do mine. Thou needst not fear my stay
   While such a bond of sympathy remains
I will not harm thee; I will never play
The kidnapper, and rifle thee away
   For ever from thy native hawthorn lanes;
   Rob thee of freedom till thy dying day,
Far from thy sorrowing mate; and while thy pains
Wring from thy ebon breast sweet plaintive strains
   Gloat o'er the wrongs that on thy spirit weigh!
Life, love, and liberty thou shalt not lack,
Nor be my slave because thy hue is black.

Tenth Month 9th, 1846.—This day my poem on
"The Death of Clarkson," is published in the *Patriot*
and in the *Suffolk Chronicle.* He was a man of great
eminence as a philanthropist, who, by his enor
mous labours, and with some hazard of his life, did
more than any other man to abolish the negro slave
trade between Africa and the West Indies. He may,

indeed, be looked upon as the great originator of
the art of agitation as a means of effecting important public objects, by stirring up the conscience,
and the common sense of the nation, without the
dangerous aid of physical force; and thus effecting
great moral and political revolutions. It is to this
system of patiently and persistently working out
great results by organised agitation, that England
owes much of her influence and prosperity as a
nation.

ODE ON THE DEATH OF THOMAS CLARKSON.

Be my rude hand inspired,
That once touched Clarkson's righteous hand with joy,
While I my harp employ,
Deep in these solemn woodland shades retired.
Freedom has lost her dauntless pioneer!—
One of those strong-armed axe-men who are born
The tangled path of common men to clear—
A herald of the evangelic morn,
When every chain that cramps the human mind
Shall disappear—
Shall fall asunder, powerless to bind,
Like the green withs round Samson's limbs entwined!
For, as the Danite rose from slumbers deep,
The nations shall awake, as out of sleep,
And shake themselves from error, and behold,
Borne on the winds that round the world shall sweep,
The mists of ages from before them rolled!
The shackles of the mind
Wait to be burst some future glorious day;
But those which served the negro's limbs to bind
Are cast for ever away!

And he whose honourable course is run,
Who raised in youth the banner of the slave,
Ceased not his toils, nor sank into his grave,
    Till the great work was done;
But like a soldier, ere his setting sun,
    Saw the great victory won!

    When men go off Life's stage,
Their actions form their monument
    To every distant age.
The chief; whom nothing can content
    And nothing can deter,—
A pestilential conqueror,
On power and plunder bent,
Round whose triumphant chariot wheels
The blood of half the world congeals,—
With whom, to hurl a monarch down,
And give away his conquered crown,
    Is but imperial play;
What monument, I ask, of true renown,
Remains of him when he has passed away?
None! None, compared with his whose loftier mind
Looks only to the good of all mankind;
Who spurns the pomp that conquest might bestow,
    And, urged by zeal profuse,
Toils with unslackened ardour, to reduce
    The sum of human woe,
To wipe the tears that never ought to flow,
    And let the captive go.

When such a being to the dust returns;
When the weak bulrush bends its trembling head;
When the lamp feebly in its socket burns,
And snow upon the mountain-top is spread;
    When the sun's light has fled,

And pipe, and harp, and lute, in vain
· Attempt their smooth clear notes again,
And every ivory key is snapt in twain—
Yes ! when the torch of life expiring lies,
    Why should we shed a tear ?
Poor is the recompense which earth supplies
    For man's best actions here ;
    And therefore when he dies,
We rather should rejoice than idly mourn,
Because—redeemed, and freed from worldly ties—
His disembodied spirit is upborne,
    Above all tears, all sighs,
To find that best reward—that glorious prize—
    A crown beyond the skies !

Emancipated spirit ! wing thy way
Amid the golden chalices of light,
Onward and onward to the realms of day !
Oh, what rare visions burst upon thy sight!
What joys, new kindling, glad thee with their
    ray !
    Thy toils are o'er !
Earth's anxious cares disturb thy peace no more !
    Thy task is done !
Thy objects thou hast lived to see
    Accomplished one by one !
And now from bad men's hatred free,
    Thy triumph has begun !
And lo ! ten thousand of the blest—
The once enslaved, the once oppressed—
Come sailing through the blue immense
    Around thy path to wait,
And with a holy violence
    Escort thee through Heaven's gate,

Saying, " Rejoice ! the weary chain,
That bound thee to the earth, is burst in twain !
And thou art come at length to Zion's height !
    For ever now made free.
Thine is the perfect liberty
    Of the blest saints in light !
'Tis thine the songs of Zion to recite !
    'Tis thine to walk in white ! "

CHAPTER XI.

Trip to Cumberland and Westmorland — "Alone upon Helvellyn" — "Spirit Musings"—Peace Congress at Paris—Tour in Switzerland—Excursion with Samuel Fennell to the Highlands of Scotland—Trip to Mull, Staffa, and Iona.

IN the summer of 1848, I enjoyed the pleasure of visiting the beautiful scenery of Westmorland and Cumberland. The mountains, the valleys, the lakes, and waterfalls of those romantic regions afforded me a rapturous delight, having been accustomed only to the rockless but fertile fields of Essex. I had no companion either to share my enthusiasm, or to divert my thoughts.

One morning I mounted the coach at Ambleside, on my way to Keswick; and finding two young men were about to climb Helvellyn, I dismounted, and asked them whether they would allow me to accompany them.

My companions, I found, were more accustomed to mountain-climbing than myself, and soon outstripped me. I kept them in sight, however, for not a tree or a shrub obstructed the view. I overtook them at last, as they stood by the little cairn on the top of the mountain just by the edge of the abrupt and fearful precipice beyond it. There they soon left me all to myself, for they proceeded down the narrow, dangerous path called Striden-edge, with a

precipice on each side of it, which leads by Blea
Tarn to the valley far below.   It was from this
narrow and dangerous path that poor young Gough
fell and perished, as related in Sir Walter Scott's
poem.

I watched them in their perilous descent till they
were out of sight, and then abandoned myself to the
enjoyment of my glorious solitude amidst the grand
scenery around me.

ALONE UPON HELVELLYN.

Alone upon Helvellyn's top,
   I lingered six ecstatic hours,
Above the pathway of the clouds,
   Beyond the fountains of the showers.

Methought, while slowly labouring up,
   " If such my toil to climb so high,
What but the shoulders of a God
   Upheaved this mountain to the sky!"

This battle-ground of wintry storms
   The summer sunbeams now caressed;
The air was like an infant's sigh
   That dreams upon its mother's breast.

Cloud-shadows softly mottled o'er
   The lesser mountains far away,
That, stretching out their rugged forms,
   Like wearied giants, slumbering, lay.

The earth seemed narrowed to a point—
   I stood upon its lofty crown,
The world was all beneath my feet
   On which, in triumph, I looked down.

The abodes of men far out of sight—
Unelbowed by the human race—
I seemed earth's sole inhabitant,
   With Heaven alone brought face to face

My spirit bounded with the joy
   Of freedom from all worldly care,
The weight of harass and of pain,
   That lower mortals have to bear.

Half-way to Heaven, without a cloud
   Between me and the realms divine,
The home of purity and peace,
   For which the weary-hearted pine.

And, as I thither raised my eyes,
   The rapturous wish inspired my breast—
" O, for the pinions of a dove,
   To flee away and be at rest ! "

The mountain-tops are hallowed ground,
   An open house of prayer and praise,
By prophets' and by patriarchs' feet
   Made holy in the ancient days.

E'en God Himself, on Sinai's mount,
   Midst cloud and flame gave forth His law
While thunders, lightnings, and the sound
   Of trumpet filled all hearts with awe.

And Christ His future glorious reign
   Clearly revealed to mortal sight
When in the Holy Mount He stood,
   Transfigured in the cloud of light.

No marvel that primeval man,
  In heathen ignorance undone,
Worshipped, upon those mountain-tops,
  The god of fire—the rising sun.

In the dim ages of the past,
  Far midst the pre-historic times,
When Pagan priests to enhance their power,
  Struck terror with their hideous crimes.

Perhaps upon this lofty ridge
  The mystic fire at midnight shone;
And human victims died the death,
  Or down this gulf were headlong thrown.

How wondrous are the steadfast hills!
  Are they not calendars sublime?
Doubtless the gauge of starry space
  Is equalled by the gauge of time!

The infinite, eternal God,
  . His sovereign purpose to fulfil,
In fashioning this complex world,
  With grand delay worked out His will.

Haply ten thousand ages past,
  This crag has reared its forehead grey;
The first to greet the quickening dawn,
  The last to part with dying day.

But what from olden time has been,
  Will not, and shall not, always be;
A marvellous change awaits the world,
  And sin and sorrow soon shall flee.

Erelong the mountains shall bring peace;
The dayspring from on high shall shine;
And gloriously the mountain tops
Shall redden with the rays divine!

SPIRIT MUSINGS.

Earth, who made thee?
Who could the great Geometrician be?
If we should seek Him where shall He be found?
Who measured out thy depth and breadth and length,
    And girded thee with strength?
Who spread abroad the waters of the sea,
And builded up a rampart and a bound
    O'er which they should not pass?
Who forged thy bands of iron and of brass?
    Who formed thy ribs of rock?
Who chiselled them from out the solid block?
Who clothed thee in habiliments so fair?
Who balanced thee on nothing in thin air,
    And bade thee run
The circuit of the far off fiery sun?
    Earth! who made thee?
    Earth answers, " God made me!"
Yes, God the High and Holy One,
    Almighty God made thee!
And thereby thus His Sovereign Power displayed;
His voice commanded and the world was made,
    He spake, and it was done!

How lovely must the youthful earth have been
    In its first flush of beauty, when the glow
Of adolescence wrapped each peaceful scene;
    And hill, and hanging grove, and lake below

M

Glittered each one
In the new-kindled, ether-burning sun!
When the pure air
Sparkled throughout the firmament serene,
A cloudless firmament for ever fair!
And tree and flower
Put forth the tender leaf of delicate green
Lustrous with dew, ere earth had known a shower;
Whilst gay enamoured birds of various notes
Warbling sweet strains from their melodious throats,
And odoriferous winds, sighing along
The sylvan solitudes their dreamy song,
And brooks, forth-leaping from their moss retreats
With graceful bounds,
Made earth one pleasant scene of sights and sounds,
A wilderness of sweets!

God spake and earth was made!
But man He formed with His own hands divine;
Man is God's workmanship, God's own design,
In God's own image fashioned and arrayed;
Let God be ever worshipped and obeyed!
God formed and fashioned him from out the dust,
Therefore in dust let human pride be laid.
The Lord God formed him of the dust of the ground
That in his own deserts he should not trust,
But that whatever in his make were found
Of good, or fair, or amiable, or just,
To God alone the glory should redound!
In His own perfect image man he made,
And over all
Dominion gave him, and unlimited power,
And placed him free to stand, or "free to fall."

Alas! in evil hour
The mandate of his God he disobeyed,
And from his high original—his state
Of innocence, and Eden's blissful bower—
Offending fell; his faculties decayed,
And his first heavenly nature, which so late
Beamed with seraphic beauty in his face,
Faded, and passed away, and in its place
Raged passions, whereof worst were pride and hate;
The signs—sad signs of downfall, and disgrace,
And ruin to his race!

The Eternal Father all events foreknows:
Some He permits, and some He foreordains.
Ere the first morning rose
Man, and whatever unto man pertains,
The Omniscient eye of God foresaw: He saw
The end from the beginning! Yes, God saw
Man's downfall, and permitted it, and chose
His plan for man's redemption from Death's law,
Even the death of Christ, whose death should draw
The sting from death, and endless life disclose!
Man was created free,
Endued with power successfully to oppose,
And rendered able to defeat the aim
Of the arch-fiend, whate'er his shape might be,
And warned of danger, and retributive woes,
If he should eat of the forbidden tree.
His Maker our first parent could not blame,
But only bow
His face to earth and kiss his kindred dust
In deep humility, and conscious shame,
And, with sincerity of heart, allow
That God is just!

But wherefore God permitted man to fall
      Is not revealed ;
Nor why, for one man's sin, death fell on all.
God, in His sacred wisdom, has concealed
      From finite man
The scope and full circumference of His plan.
      Deep things belong to Him ;
While round ourselves mysterious clouds are rolled.
Our light comes through a crevice in the wall,
And we, like atoms, in the sunbeam swim !
So when the prophet Daniel of old,
By Babylon's broad river was foreshown
By an angel what far ages should unfold
Of monarchies built up and overthrown,
And caught faint glimpses of the dim unknown,
He heard and saw but could not comprehend :
      Then was he told
The words were sealed even unto the end.
Thus are we left enwrapt in mystery
      Until the end shall be ;
But when the long-predicted end shall be
      Then, then our eyes shall see !

How strong is human reason !   Yet how weak !
      Weak beyond lips to speak !
Strong as a giant in its rightful sphere,
But feeble as a babe in things divine,
Searching the realms of Nature far and near,
But stumbling blindfold in the Spirit-mine.
At Truth's strong door in vain may Reason knock,
      The key of Revelation can alone
      The door of Truth unlock ;
And Truth alone can turn the golden key
      Of Heavenly mystery,

And sacred things to finite man make known !
But Reason, self-sufficient, stands aloof
And gazing up at Heaven's miraculous roof
Dares to throw scorn on faith, and asks for *proof !*
The sceptic, like an ape in a balloon,
      Soars up into the air,
Betwixt the solid earth and doubtful moon,
      Drifting he knows not where ;
Grinning and chattering, and with eyes a-scare,
      And trembling with affright,
Impelled by aimless winds, now here, now there,
O'er ocean's depth, or mountains' barren height.
Through blinding mists, or up through regions rare
Of gorgeous cloudland, dazzling to the sight,
To be precipitated all too soon,
      Down headlong to the ground,
To fill a little common grassy mound—
      Death's secret found !

Faith is "the evidence of things not seen,"
      A supernatural sense
      Given by Omnipotence,
Confirming what shall be by what has been,
      In sure and certain hope serene—
      A principle of power,
By which the illuminated human soul
Can read and understand the sacred scroll,
      And antedate,
      With holy joy elate,
E'en in this brief probationary state,
      Yea, in the darkest hour,
Those great and precious promises of Heaven
      Which in that scroll are given—

The advent of that bright and gladsome day,
　　Come when it may,
For which from childhood and unsullied youth
　　Our lips are taught to pray,
And saints in every age have striven—
Christ's glorious kingdom ! full of grace and truth,
And love, and light, and joy, and peace, and rest ;
　　When Mercy shall alone bear sway,
　　And none shall be oppressed ;
When death and darkness shall afar be driven,
And when all sin, all woe, all pain, all doubt,
　　Shall be stamped out ;
All tears for evermore be wiped away,
　　And all mankind be blessed.

Eighth Month 21st, 1849.—Left London for Paris
to attend the Peace Congress held in the Salle St.
Cécile. Victor Hugo was called to the chair. His
opening speech was animated and eloquent.

I was curious to notice the French style of public
speaking. There was considerable gesticulation,
particularly of the fingers, and I observed that the
emphasis was mostly laid on the last word in a
sentence, and frequently it was uttered in a higher
key. Most of the speeches were in French.

Eighth Month 25th.—Proceeded to the soirée given
to the members of the Peace Congress by the Minister
of Foreign Affairs, at his official residence in the
Boulevard des Capucines.

About 1,500 people thronged the four or five handsome rooms that were thrown open to us, or paraded
the shady little garden adjoining, which was gaily

illuminated by paper lamps of various colours suspended in the trees, or placed in little holes in the
ground. All the ministers and most of the foreign
ambassadors were present. Cobden told the Minister's
lady that so much moral worth had never been con-
gregated in that house before.

During his stay in Paris he visited many places
of interest, as the " Madeleine," " Notre Dame,"
" Louvre," and " Tuileries."

26*th.*—I took an omnibus to the Place de la·Bastille,
and then walked half a mile to the " Père la Chaise "
cemetery. It contains 100 acres, and is one of the
most interesting objects in Paris.

´ Tombs of various shapes and designs abound ; but
the humbler graves are the most remarkable. Each
is enclosed in a little wooden fence, about 4 feet long
by 3 feet wide, painted black, and is ornamented
according to the taste of the survivors. Most of
them are kept up as little gardens, with the utmost
neatness, containing roses,. china asters, and other
flowers. Generally there is a box at one end with a
glass front containing votive offerings of various
kinds, such as little images of angels, the Crucifixion,
or the Virgin Mary, or pictures of saints with sprigs
of artificial flowers, some of which were of silver, and
other little ornamental things.

In one, which was inscribed to the memory of a
little girl, there was her thimble, in another a lock of
hair ! Over most of the graves there were suspended

wreaths of yellow everlasting flowers, some of which
were inwoven with flowers dyed black, so as to form
inscriptions, such as this :

"À Notre Bon Père."

I have only room to add that, during my stay in
France, I did not observe the least indication of an
unfriendly feeling on the part of anyone. The French
people were polite and obliging, without exhibiting
anything like insincere servility; and I trust the
Peace Congress at Paris will have the effect of pro-
moting a friendly disposition between the French and
English.

Extracts from letters to his friend, B. B. Wiffen,
allude to a tour on the Continent in 1850.

"*Ninth Month* 23rd, 1850.—I returned last night from
my journey, having visited Frankfort, Basle, Berne,
Vevey, Geneva, the Vale of Chamouni, and returned by
way of Dijon to Paris."

"*Ninth Month* 29th, 1850.—Every traveller must be
delighted with Heidelburg. Bern is a charming place,
with its fine situation, its bears, its fountains, its old
streets and heavy arcades, and grotesquely dressed people.
Who can ever forget a sunset at Vevey! No one can
understand the Mer de Glace without treading it."

Eighth Month 6th, 1852.—In company with my
cousin, Samuel Fennell, I left Bury St. Edmunds,
on an excursion to the Highlands of Scotland.

At Edinburgh we ascended the long and steep ascent

to the Castle. This fine old fortress, the scene of
so many stirring events in Scottish history, greatly
interested my companion. It stands on the highest
point of the hill, and beneath it is a fearful precipice.
The view from the fortified summit is extremely fine.
We looked down on the public gardens, streets, and
churches of this picturesque city with the warmest
admiration, while in the distance we beheld the Firth
of Forth stretching far away, and the range of mountains beyond it. The atmosphere being now much
clearer, we could appreciate the charms of " Sweet
Edinboro' Town."

After surveying the lovely prospect for a considerable time, we proceeded to view the sights of the
place.

First of all we were shown Queen Mary's room
and dark and dismal enough it is, being wainscoted
with oak. Next we were shown her bedroom. There
is scarcely space in it for a modern bedstead. Here
King James I. of England was born.

The Scottish regalia, after being lost for some 200
years, was discovered—I think, by Sir Walter Scott
—a few years ago. It consists of a golden crown
(ornamented with jewels), a sword of state, two
sceptres (at the top of each of which is a round rock
crystal as large as an egg), and a magnificent golden
collar of the Order of the Garter; besides smaller
articles, most of which are adorned with precious
stones. They are kept in a small, circular room
lighted with gas, and look very brilliant. In the
same room is the huge old chest in which they
were discovered.

After breakfast we mounted the coach for Lass-
wade; and on our arrival at the village set off to
walk three miles to Hawthornden. Scotch miles
are very long, but at length we reached the entrance
gate of Hawthornden. Entering the park, we walked
down a winding drive to the mansion. Here we
found other visitors under the charge of a guide. We
joined them, and were conducted to a jutting rock,
whence it is said John Knox preached to the people
on the opposite bank of the Esk, which flows perhaps
100 ft. perpendicularly beneath one's feet—a strange
pulpit in this beautiful wilderness. This spot com-
mands an enchanting view of the wooded and rocky
banks of this winding river, and of the mansion once
inhabited by Drummond, the poet, perched on the
ivied edge of the cliff.

Passing the old tree under which Drummond and
Ben Jonson are said to have sat and conversed, we
were conducted to the entrance of a gloomy passage
cut in the solid rock. After groping our way some
distance daylight appeared again, and we came to an
opening in the face of the cliff, high above the rushing
Esk, and from which there was no exit. Lighted by
this hole in the rock was a small room, called, I
think, Sir William Wallace's cave. A huge sword
is also shown as his. In another cave is a well of
water. Altogether it is a very curious place.

Having seen the wonders of Hawthornden, our
guide dismissed us at the opposite side of the garden
to the one we entered, and we found ourselves in a
fine shady grove overlooking the Esk, and com-
manding a most beautiful view of the old mansion.

Descending to the river side, and crossing it by a foot-bridge, from which the loveliest view of all is obtained, we followed the narrow path which leads along the river to Roslyn Castle. This path is not quite two miles long, but it is so beautifully romantic, so richly adorned with wild rocks, rushing torrents, noble trees, graceful ferns, and strange flowers, that we enjoyed our ramble exceedingly. The wild raspberry, as in many other places in Scotland, grows plentifully here.

The day was now as fine as possible; and we loitered so agreeably that it must have been nearly two hours before the walls of Roslyn Castle peered above the trees. We first ascended a steep hill to the chapel. The architecture of this old ruin is, perhaps, the richest I ever beheld. The sculptures and odd designs are marvellous. Here is the famous twisted column by the apprentice of the architect who killed him out of jealousy. The sculptures, however, are greatly eaten away by time and exposure.

12th.—This morning we finally left Edinburgh, and after visiting Stirling, Dunkeld, and other places, we at length entered the famous gorge of Glencoe, which presents some of the grandest scenery in Scotland. Lofty, craggy, and dark, the mountains towered above us on either hand, bidding defiance to time and tempest. Above the top of one of the highest cliffs, we distinguished an eagle soaring, and appearing no bigger than a skylark.

Near the summit of what is called Black Mountain we saw the singular hollow which is called Ossian's Cave. It appears to be quite inaccessible. The

snow generally lies in the higher clefts of these
mountains. Near the outlet of Glencoe we passed
the scene of the famous massacre.

21st.—At seven a.m. we went on board the steamer
for Staffa and Iona. It was a fine calm day, and we
had a beautiful sail. After calling at the Isle of
Mull, we arrived about noon off the little low island
of Staffa.

Three boat-loads of passengers went ashore, on
approaching which the wonders of the place begin to
reveal themselves. We landed in a little cove where
the basaltic columns had been broken away.

How can I convey an idea of this wondrous isle?
It seemed composed of huge, black, upright, wooden
piles of all shapes and sizes fitting closely together.
The shore is composed of these columns broken off
at irregular elevations by the action of the ever-
surging sea.

We walked along this strange pathway beneath
the basaltic cliff, stepping cautiously from column to
column till we reached the Cave of Fingal. The
timid ones stayed behind. Fortunately one can creep
along the side of the cave on the flat tops of the
broken-off columns nearly to the further end. There
is a rope fixed by way of a rail.

My companion followed my leadership most man-
fully, and what a magnificent spectacle we beheld!
The cave resembles the nave of a cathedral with the
sea bellowing for ever along its rugged floor. The
arched roof is composed of the ends of the upright
columns which have been broken away, and which
ends hang overhead as if they were ready to fall.

Having lingered half an hour in this extraordinary cavern, we cautiously retraced our steps, and returned to the steamer in high spirits at our adventures. Fingal's Cave is 227 ft. long, 40 ft. broad, and 60 ft. high.

In about an hour we arrived at the low sterile island of Iona. We landed in boats on the sea-weedy rocks, and were instantly beset by children with little shells for sale. We visited the ruins of the old monastery, and also those of the cathedral, all of simple primitive architecture.

In the graveyard are one or two old sculptured crosses, also the effigied tombstones of some of the old kings and bishops of Scotland. A guide conducted us about ; but the crumbling walls and quaint old tombstones speak best for themselves.

Once more embarked we proceeded homewards round the south side of Mull, which presents an unusually barren specimen of rocky splendour.

It was a lovely evening when we returned to the picturesque bay of Oban. Passing the Kyles of Bute, and entering the Firth of Clyde, we landed at Bowling for Loch Lomond.

At Inversnaid we took coach and proceeded through one of the wildest districts in Scotland, five miles to Loch Katrine, passing the grim ruins of an old castle by the way. We were set down at the new inn at the lower end of the Loch, where we had to wait an hour for the steamer. It was crowded with passengers. We sailed slowly up the romantic Loch ten miles; the upper end is superlatively beautiful and grand. The mountains above the woodlands

were richly tinted with the "blooming heather,"
which added greatly to the effect.

Passed through the famous wooded defile called
the Trosachs, which are flanked by lofty mountains
and extend about a mile. Here we saw one of the
wild deer of Scotland. It was as red as a brick.

They returned home by way of Stirling, Lanark,
and Glasgow, arriving at Bury St. Edmunds on the
28th.

A sonnet to one of Scotland's great poets may here
be introduced.

TO BURNS.

There are more wrecks on thy enchanted shore,
Sweet Poesy ! than on the rocks that guard
Cape Horn's terrific coast, where winds blow hard,
And waves their everlasting thunders roar.
Poor Burns ! thou child of Inspiration, bard
Of eagle intellect, and fate ill-starred !
Thy strains shall live though thou art seen no more.
The soldier, far away, in battle scarred—
The shepherd-boy, roaming the mountains o'er—
The sailor, clinging to the mainmast yard
Each fond enthusiast holds thee in regard,
And cheers his spirit with thy tuneful lore.
May I, though tossed upon the self-same sea,
Escape the rocks that made a wreck of thee.

CHAPTER XII.

Footpath Association—Gladstone and the Corn Laws—French
Treaty—" England and France " — Sonnet to " Bracy
Clark, F.L.S."—D. W. Harvey—Curious *rencontre* in a
stage coach—Death of Cobden—Sonnet to " Richard
Cobden "—Death of his father.

Fifth Month 14th, 1856.—Public meeting to preserve
the cross paths in Cooke's Field. Received a vote of
thanks for my services as Secretary of the Footpath
Association. Spirited meeting !

Second Month 18th, 1859.—Grand Footpath Meeting
at the Town Hall, to prevent the inclosure of the
Castle Bailey.

Eleventh Month 11th, 1859.—It is all over with my
dear cousin, Jane Clark. She died on the 3rd inst.
After settling some outward affairs, her work being
accomplished and her mind at ease, she sank apparently to sleep. But presently she opened her eyes
again, and uttered these remarkable words, " What
a grand company ! " Her aged father says it was a
view of the heavenly blessed ones. She then closed
her eyes again, and in a few minutes ceased to breathe.
I went to London on the 9th to attend the funeral.
It was a sad day indeed to me.

Second Month 11th, 1860.—Last night Gladstone,
the Chancellor of the Exchequer, brought forward

his budget in an eloquent speech, carrying out whole-
sale the great principles of Free Trade.

At the same time Cobden's treaty with the Emperor
of the French was discussed. These great measures
are of unbounded importance. France and England
will be united by the bonds of commerce and the
ties of mutual interest.

To the long-suffering members of the much-abused
Anti-Corn Law League it is a glorious consummation
of their labours, anxieties, and aims.

ENGLAND AND FRANCE.

Shake hands ! shake hands ! let us be friends ;
    Shake hands ! let us forget the past ;
Hope's bow from shore to shore extends,
    A glorious day has dawned at last.
Nations that would be wise and great,
    With all the world must coalesce,
'Tis bad alike for man or state
    To live in single blessedness.
Shake hands ! and may the dreadful battle-roar
Of England and of France be heard no more !

Twelfth Month 16th, 1860.—This day my dear uncle,
Bracy Clark, F.L.S., a noted veterinary surgeon, died,
aged nearly ninety years.

A few weeks before his death he sold the skeleton
of the famous race-horse, " Eclipse," to the Veterinary College of Edinburgh. I have often seen it in
the study, some years ago, and heard him expatiate
on the wonderful horse.

TO BRACY CLARK, F.L.S.

Descendant not unworthy of a sire !
The Hampden of the common where he dwelt,
Bracy, this tribute of a deep, heartfelt,
And honest admiration, I desire
To offer to thy name. The world has dealt
Unkindly with thee ; and the heart must melt
To see a genius, which could not tire,
Cramped, like the hoof within its iron belt.
But so it is ; the dead, whom we admire,
At whose proud tombs past centuries have knelt,
Were, when alive, the men the world could pelt,
And see in chains or banishment expire.
One comfort still remains to gild our earth,
Men cannot crush the consciousness of worth.

Tenth Month 1st, 1861.—This is a great day for
England. The paper duty expires, and knowledge
is untaxed.

First Month 13th, 1862.—My father got down stairs
yesterday and dined, but was glad to get to bed again.
Whenever he is drowsy his mind wanders. He is
a source of constant care and anxiety. He is very
feeble, and requires our frequent assistance. There
seems no immediate danger, but it is hardly likely
he can recover at his great age of 87. Happily his
mind is in perfect peace as regards the future.

First Month 5th, 1863. — Another stage of life's
journey begun. My father still occupies my daily
care. Nothing like conversation now passes between
us. I can make him understand little else but " Yes "
and " No." But he still fights bravely with old age.

N

He still posts the books, and walks his daily mile in the garden when it is fine.

Third Month 4th, 1863.—Daniel Whittle Harvey died recently. He was one of the greatest, if not the greatest, orator of his day. I knew him well as member for Colchester. He died rather suddenly, aged 77. When my father lived at Boreham, in the early part of this century, he had occasion one day to go to London by the Coggeshall coach. As the weather was cold, he travelled inside. Three gentlemen occupied the other seats, two of whom were elderly, and the third was young.

One of the senior gentlemen and the other who sat opposite to him had a great deal of conversation together as they journeyed along. They talked on various subjects both foreign and domestic; and, having exhausted the politics of the day, proceeded to discuss the affairs of their acquaintance.

After a little pause one of them exclaimed, "What do you think of young Harvey?" This question referred to a speech at a political meeting at Maldon, which D. W. Harvey had recently made, which had electrified his audience by its polished eloquence, and had created a great sensation in the country.

The question was answered by the opposite gentleman in a very depreciatory manner. He ridiculed the presumption of the ambitious young orator in no measured terms. He said that young Harvey had actually been seen making a speech before a looking-glass, and throwing his arms about in the most absurd manner; and he concluded his comments on the young aspirant for political distinction by boldly prophesying that such a shallow young fellow would never succeed in making any figure in the world.

My father and his opposite neighbour sat silent, and listened to all that was said without joining in the conversation, which soon changed to other subjects. After a while the coach stopped at Romford to change horses. There was another pause in the conversation.

The elderly gentleman who had been expressing his opinions very freely about Harvey looked across towards the young man, who sat opposite my father, rather earnestly, and said, " I think, Sir, I have seen you before, though I cannot recollect where." " Then I'll tell you," said the young man, in a strong, ringing, voice ; " I had the honour of dining with you a few weeks ago, at Mr. Honeywood's." The elderly gentleman, lifting up his hands, as if in amazement, exclaimed, " Mr. Harvey ! " His embarrassment may be readily imagined. However, he extended his hand to the young man, and professed his pleasure at meeting him again.

My father, in relating this anecdote, always expressed his admiration at the reticence of young Harvey, who made not the slightest allusion to the description of himself to which, in this odd manner, he had just had the privilege of listening.

Eighth Month 3rd, 1864.—Our housekeeper, Elizabeth Mead, who has lived with us since the year 1835, is almost worn out with labour and anxiety. Her efforts to make my deaf father hear seem to have produced a throat complaint and affection of the tongue.

She died a few months afterwards, an example of true devotedness.

Fourth Month 3rd, 1865.—Yesterday died Richard Cobden, the greatest benefactor of modern England. Knowing him so intimately, I have felt the sad event as the loss of a private friend.

TO RICHARD COBDEN.

Cobden, thy battles for the common good
Are noble! bringing rival nations near
In commerce, amity, and prosperous cheer;
And proving how divine is brotherhood.
Thy victories leave behind no scars—or worse,
Restrictive laws, deep debt, and want severe.
Immortal song such triumphs should rehearse.
What good was Waterloo? It was a curse,
Which since has filled our land with secret fear
Of vengeance, and invasion, and reverse;
And wrung a kingdom's ransom, year by year,
In hard-earned millions from the people's purse.
Napoleon rules in France!—Poor Wellington
Lived to behold his well-paid work undone!

First Month 7th, 1866.—My poor father is much worse; I think now he is really going.

11*th*.—My father is no more. A heavenly smile illumined his features ere he breathed his last breath without a sigh or a struggle. A week before he died the nurse tells me he said to her, "My time is short. Thank the Lord on my account that I am forewarned; that I am so far towards Heaven."

On the First - day before he died he said to her,
" When will the Lord please to take me ? May I die
praising the Lord ! " And when the end drew near,
the words, " Lord Jesus " were the last which he
faintly uttered.

18th.—Yesterday I followed my father to his grave.
Good old Joseph Shewell spoke at the grave, and
Jonathan Grubb most beautifully in the meeting
afterwards. A memorable day indeed !

Fifth Month 31st.—Next quarter-day I am to give
up business and leave these premises. Meanwhile
the liberty which I used to long for has lost its
charms. All my dearest friends are dead, and I feel
that I am about to go forth into the world a lonely
stranger, not knowing what may befall me. My hope
and trust for help and guidance are in the Divine
Arm, which has hitherto protected me.

CHAPTER XIII.

He leaves Colchester — Various wanderings — Returns to
Kelvedon—His marriage—Settlement at Colchester—
Publication of the " Setting Sun "—"Lines on St.
Botolph's Priory, Colchester " — Birth of his son —
Removal to Lexden—"Lexden Springs"—"My Garden,"
by L. B. Hurnard—Visits British Association Meetings—
Extracts from a poem and prose, by Thomas Lister—
" The Land's End "—" Dirge on the Burial of Living-
stone in Westminster Abbey."

" Loving and faithful, even unto death !
        Well may it falter
The lip this solemn promise as it saith
        Before that altar,
Where, o'er the trembling covenanters lean
Recording Angel and High Priest unseen.

" Loving and faithful, what is it to be
        Now and forever ?
The heart is asking, as it puts to sea
        To turn back never,
If it can keep the promise of to-day
In its full meaning, sacred and alway.

" Loving and faithful while a boundless reach
        Of spotless azure
O'erarches hearts too full for common speech
        Their bliss to measure ;
Loving and faithful when the first clouds lie
In rolls of silvered fleece along the sky.

" Loving and faithful, while existence fills
     With joy o'erflowing,
While in their faces sweet airs from the hills
     Of morn are blowing,
And when loud storm-winds have their own
     wild will,
Wrapping their vow around them closer still."

E. LLOYD, Jun.

AFTER this period, the account in the note books
not being sufficiently complete, I have taken up the
thread of the narrative of my dear husband's life.
He left Colchester on the 23rd of Sixth Month, 1866,
for Lowestoft, thence on a visit to relatives at Great
Yarmouth, and for some time made his home with
his cousins, Dr. and C. Pope, in London, whence he
visited various places ; amongst others he stayed at
Woburn with his literary friend B. B. Wiffen, from
whose dictation he wrote down a narrative respecting
the Spanish Reformers (in whose writings B. B.
Wiffen had felt great interest), " snatching it, as
it were, from the grave's mouth," as B. B. Wiffen
died shortly afterwards.

After nearly a year spent in various wanderings, he
went into lodgings at Kelvedon, Essex, and here a
great change took place in his experience.

He became engaged to one whom he had known
from her childhood, Louisa Bowman Smith, daughter
of his old friend Louisa Bowman, who had married
Charles Smith, of Coggeshall. The mother had

long since passed away, and the father had removed
to Kelvedon.

It was on the 15th of Eighth Month, 1867, that
we were married at the Friends' Meeting-house
Kelvedon, when, in the simple but beautiful language
of the Friends' marriage ceremony, each promised to
be unto the other " loving and faithful, until it shall
please the Lord by death to separate us."

There was a good sized family gathering, and
amongst those present was the brother, Charles
Edward Smith, a young surgeon, who had recently
returned from his perilous voyage amid the Arctic
Seas, where, unprovisioned for a winter, the ship had
been ice-bound, and the crew had suffered great hardships.

Providentially the ice broke up early that spring,
and the leaky vessel, with its cargo of dead and
living, was permitted to reach Shetland.   It seemed
as if the wind blew it just to its desired haven, and
my brother was alive to tell the tale.

Eight of that family gathering since then have
passed away.

> " As happy married couples often do,
> Away we hasted to the Isle of Wight,
> That paradise of newly-wedded pairs.
> We rambled on the sands of calm Sea View,
> We visited the grave of Little Jane,
> We sauntered up sweet shady Shanklin Chine,
> We roamed about the lovely Undercliff,
> We clambered up the steep St. Boniface,

And lingered long on Ventnor's sheltered sands.
'Twas fine to sit upon the soft sea beach,
And idly watch the busy waves at work ;
With Neptune's wife 'tis always washing-day.
Grand was the flashing moonlight on the deep,
And bright the sunshine on the breezy downs :
So passed with speed our joyful honeymoon."
                    From " The Setting Sun."

One day as we walked back from Luccombe Chine
to Shanklin along the smooth sandy beach, resting
on the boulders and admiring the grand cliffs, my
eye was attracted by a fossil shell protruding from
near the base of one of the hard black rocks, and I
went to examine it, and see whether it would leave
its hard bed; but this was out of the question.

Just at this time I heard a deep booming sound,
and then we were startled by a sudden crash ! Down
came a body of earth and rock at only a few yards
distance from us ! It was enough apparently to have
crushed us had we not paused to look at the shell,
which, in its hard bed where it had rested for ages,
was thus providentially made the means of our pre-
servation.

Our trembling hearts were filled with admiring
gratitude !

After some weeks passed amid the lovely scenes of
that beautiful island we settled at Colchester, first in
lodgings, and then in a comfortable home in Head
Street ; and here my husband was much engaged in
continuing and completing a long poem which he had

commenced at Great Yarmouth for the sake of occupation, and to escape from his tried feelings during his wandering life. It was entitled "The Setting Sun," and was eventually published during the winter of 1869-70. Opinions as to its merits were various. It is a very original poem, "quaint and vigorous," and "abounds in passages of true poetry."

He felt great interest in the improvement and welfare of the old town of Colchester, which had been his home for so many years, in the election of its Borough Members, of its Town Council, and in the improvement of its Town Hall.

A poem on one of its fine old ruins may here be introduced :—

LINES ON ST. BOTOLPH'S PRIORY, COLCHESTER.

The moon looks on thee, desolated pile!
   She, who beheld thee in thine ancient glory;
Her face has not yet lost its youthful smile,
   Nor are her golden locks grown thin or hoary;
No! still she reigns the sovereign of the night
The poet's patron and the lover's light.

But thou art of those sublunary things
   On which the hand of Time delights to revel;
That hand which hurls down monarchies and kings,
   And lays the Babylons of ages level;
That blights the blooming rose on beauty's cheek,
And bids old age its last asylum seek.

Gigantic skeleton of splendour past,
  Roofless and gateless court of superstition,
Standing all open to the bleak night blast,
  Unconscious of thy desolate condition,
What revolutions in the lapse of time
Have changed the world since thou wast in thy prime!

Winters on winters round thy walls have blown,
  A thousand storms have spent their anger on thee;
The sunshine-smiles of summer thou hast known,
  Chill frost, and rain, and snow, have fall'n upon thee;
Winds that have borne infection in their breath
Have whistled through thy crumbling arches " death."

King Henry's spoiling hand, with rapine red,
  Assailed thee in the zenith of thy splendour;
And that wild storm that broke on Charles's head
  Burst upon thee, and rent thy walls asunder.
Thou the stern wrath of haughty Fairfax bore;
But tremble not—his arm is strong no more!

On thy raised threshold Desolation sits
  And wistfully surveys thy broken arches;
For her too harmlessly each moment flits,
  And with too slow a pace Time onward marches—
She loves the ship fast bilging on the shore,
The sudden earthquake, the wild battle roar.

High on these dark, yet moon-illumined walls,
  That once were clad with many a decoration,
The tall grass trembles and the bramble crawls,
  And sparrows make their peaceful habitation;
And oft the ghostly owl, supplied with food,
Through the dim air flies homeward to its brood.

Here the green ivy wraps thy columns round,
  And there, along from arch to arch, reposes.
Thy capitals, with youth and beauty crowned,
  Smile as a death's head in a wreath of roses.
Fond plant, these walls thus richly to array
And hide the ruin which thou canst not stay!

Along these aisles no monk now slowly treads—
  Dumb is the solemn voice of supplication;
No flaming altar round its incense sheds
  No flaring torch gleams on the rich oblation;
But, through the mutilated archway nigh,
Streams the pale moonbeam from its fount on high.

Thou placid moon, fair sovereign of the night,
  Unclasp the tire that binds thy golden tresses,
Shine forth with all thy beams and put to flight
  The gloom that reigns in these profound recesses;
Shine on this lonely spot with grass o'erspread,
And soothe the slumbers of the dreamy dead.

Haply, when darkness fills the midnight sky,
  Here to and fro the ghost of Ernulph ranges,
Or leans upon some massive column nigh,
  To muse upon the world and all its changes,
Mourn o'er the fortunes of the Papal crown,
Abbeys profaned, and altars broken down;

To sigh—" Alas of man it is the fate
  To triumph one short hour, and then to perish!
Empires have but a transitory date—
  All that man grasps at—all that fond hearts cherish!
What wonder then if thou art swept away
Thou hoary pile, of Time the helpless prey.

" E'en royal Rome herself is mouldering fast !
Her domes fall prostrate like the broken bubble,
Her ruined walls look up to Heaven aghast,
And all her strength is as autumnal stubble ;
And well for her if lightnings winged with power
Assail her not and whelm her in an hour.

" Time — on whose shoulders huge the world is
    borne—
E'en Time grows feeble and his locks are frosted ;
Himself erelong—insensate, blind, and worn—
Shall throw his burden down like one exhausted—
Shall, with a sigh, his comrade Death dismiss,
And sink into Eternity's abyss ! "

It was on the 17th of Eighth Month, 1870, that
our domestic happiness was crowned by the birth of
our only son, who was named Samuel Fennell. With
what joy did the father watch the unfolding of the
physical and mental powers of his infant son !
What a contrast to the lonely life he so long had
led !

Amid joys and sorrows, the lot of man, our quiet
life flowed on, varied generally in summer by a stay
at the sea-side, which we loved so well, till, having
inherited a considerable accession to his means, on
the longest day in 1873, we took up our residence
in a lovely country home in Lexden, not far from
Colchester. Here my husband enjoyed the country
walks of which a favourite one was to Lexden
Springs, which inspired his muse.

LEXDEN SPRINGS.

1829.

I stood by Lexden Springs to hear
　The music of the murmuring rill;
The skies above were calm and clear
　And all the world around was still.
Sad thoughts within my breast arose,
　As by the brook I listening stood,
To see that men to men are foes—
　To see that man delights in blood

The stars were lit, the moon was up,
　And though the elms her lustre cast;
"O, where," said I, " will avarice stop?
　How long will man's ambition last?
O, why has man so dark a mind?
　O, why has man so hard a heart?
He has the power to bless mankind,
　Yet plays the ignoble tyrant's part!"

A little foot-bridge spans the stream;
　I leaned against the oaken rail,
And watched the rippling waters gleam,
　And muttered, "What can hope avail?
Want sheds the sad, beseeching tear,
　And sorrow lifts the broken prayer;
But Pride stalks by, unheeding here;
　Oppression, blindfold, marches there.

"O, would the sons of men were wise—
　Would mind the warnings of the past—
And learn that all that bad men prize
　Turns but to loss and dross at last!"

The clock now struck the hour of e'en
　Its voice forbade my longer stay;
I left behind the peaceful scene,
　But took my grief of heart away.

1876.

Twice twenty years, and more, have passed
　Since I composed that plantive song,
·Athwart those years my gaze I cast,
　With feelings deep and pulses strong.
This brook still keeps its onward way,
　It knows no round returning track!
And of those years not one short day
　Will unrelenting Time bring back!

The foot-bridge still, though sore decayed,
　Bestrides the gentle rippling stream,
And, midst the elm trees' leafy shade,
　The moon and stars still sweetly gleam :
But on an altered world they shine—
　Loud neighs the railway's fiery steed,
And words along the electric line
　Flash to and fro with lightning speed.

Science has changed the phase of life,
　But man is human as of yore;
And passions which engender strife
　Have plunged the East and West in gore.
Ambition, Pride, and love of gain
　Still rage within man's guilty breast;
While humble merit strives in vain,
　And honest worth toils on depressed.

But I am happier than in youth;
   With wider views I wait "that day"
Predicted in the Page of Truth,
   When Right o'er all men shall bear s way!
When He who is the King of kings,
   Shall come in glory from the skies,
And sweeten all earth's bitter springs,
   And make our world one Paradise.

A lovely garden, too, afforded him much enjoyment, having it well planted with fruit trees, and
watching their growth with interest.

Some domestic verses, which I gave him on one
of his birthdays, written as if by himself, describe
some of these enjoyments.

MY GARDEN.

The silver hairs were flowing
   My youth and prime were past,
I left the noisy, busy town,
   And found a home at last
Within sweet Lexden's peaceful glades,
   Where floats the balmy air;
And I can walk, and think, and talk
   Within my garden fair,
      My garden, my garden,
   Within my garden fair.

Oh pleasant are the strolls I take !
   Refreshing is the breeze !
The summer sun can harm me not
   Beneath the chestnut trees;

And when the Autumn tints the leaves
    With colours rich and rare,
A golden shower falls all around
    Within my garden fair,
                My garden, &c.

The rooks are busy o'er my head
    With cheerful noisy caw;
And as I walked beneath the firs
    A pheasant fine I saw;
And once I heard young Thomas shout
    And up there jumped a hare!
I love to see each living thing
    Within my garden fair,
                My garden, &c.

Upon the gravel path so trim
    The beech-nuts falling fast,
I look aloft, and in the tree
    ,A squirrel spy at last!
It runs along and leaps so quick
    From bough to bough with care,
'Tis welcome to a meal and home
    Within my garden fair,
                My garden, &c.

But most I love to see our boy
    Brimful of life and fun
With ball, or stick, or wheelbarrow,
    About the garden run;
With Finch and Florrie by his side,
    Happy and free from care
How many joyous hours they spend
    Within my garden fair,
                My garden, &c.

O

His mother, too, when skies are bright,
  And winds are soft and calm,
Delights to share my walk and talk
  Leaning upon my arm;
Or on the lawn, beneath the shade,
  Will take her basket-chair,
And drink in health and happiness
  Within my garden fair,
          My garden, &c.

   *   *   *   *   *

How full of love our hearts should be
  To Him our Heavenly Friend,
Who placed us in this happy home,
  Such peaceful days to spend!
Oh, when our time on earth is run,
  Our work fulfilled with care,
Then may we all transplanted be
  Into His garden fair!
His garden above, where all is love,
  His perfect garden fair!

His home enjoyments were varied by occasionally attending meetings of the British Association with his poet-friend Thomas Lister and wife, of Barnsley.

Thomas Lister has given a graphic description of these visits, both in poetry and prose. The first occasion was in 1872 :—

  " At Brighton 'twas our pride to see
    And hold with Stanley converse free—
      In crowded hall to hear
    How noble Livingstone he found,
    Wandering on Afric's burning ground,
      O'er lakes and deserts drear.

" Men of all lands were gathered there,
    When Science held her 'Annual Fair,'
        And Art in splendour shone.
    There met we the Imperial three—
    Father and son since gone, and she
        To mourn them left alone.

" When Bristol, mart of shipping trade,
    The wandering *savants* welcome made
        We trod on Clifton Bridge:
    The haunts of Southey, Chatterton,
    And temple-shrines we gaz'd upon,
        And climb'd the limestone ridge.

" At Plymouth wondrous arts were shown ;
    There spoke the infant telephone,
        Progressing year by year ;
    The spacious docks, the noble bays—
    Old Eddystone, which far displays
        Its light, to warn or cheer.

" The rich-veined mines of Carradon,
    The Cheese Wring on its airy throne,
        (Our portraits pictur'd there)—
    All these we saw, then journey'd far
    To where Land's End braves ocean's war
        And sea-birds scream in air."

" We had all the same wish to see the farthest
south-western lands of our native country. For
these objects we visited the Land's End, viewing
on the way the wondrous Logan Stone, which,
though many tons in weight, moved with a slight
lifting of my shoulder. On the further point of

the huge granite masses, which jut out into the
vast Atlantic, we could feel as C. Wesley so well
expresses it :—

> ' Lo, on a narrow neck of land
> Twixt two unbounded seas I stand.'

"We examined both sides of this mighty projection ;
the south-western, with the Longships Lighthouse,
and the Runnel Stone, about two miles out, and the
north-western with its tunnels and bridges formed
by the wasting action of the wild waves and other
powerful impulses of creative energy, the first inward
bend of Whitesand Bay to Cape Cornwall, 280 feet
high, its northern bound (near Botallack Mine).

"We gathered many curious specimens of ferns,
heather, lichens, and flowering plants, and admired
many more that were tantalizingly beyond our reach,
among the steep rock clefts. We can barely enume-
rate the flowers seen or gathered : the beautiful star-
wort (or Michaelmas daisy), with its yellow disc and
light purple ray, its linear lanceolated fleshy leaves,
its glabrous stem and corymbose heads ; the thrift (or
sea pink) with linear leaves and light rose-tinted
flowers.

"While some of us took light refreshment at the
cottage inscribed, ' The first and last house in
England,' or overlooked the varied specimens on
the stall in front, or watched the sea birds, the
cormorant (or shag), the ring dottrell, and gulls,
large and small, our elder companion, J. H., whose
genial nature is alike in harmony with social intercourse and occasional thoughtful solitude, retired

once more to the last point of the rocks, the base of which was washed by the deep greenish blue sea. The result of his solitary musings came out when we reached Penzance, by another route, which passed by a long-closed burial ground of the Society of Friends.

" He produced a pencilled copy of verses in which, as he expressed himself, he had endeavoured to concentrate his thoughts on the prominent but contrasted images before him,—the last bold rocks of our land and the beautiful yet inaccessible flower adorning them. I need not say that we and the company at Matthew's Temperance Hotel appreciated the brief but finished portrait of the scene, and the moral combined therewith."

THE LAND'S END.

I stood on England's furthest rock,
  That frowns defiance o'er the main,
And saw a flower within a cleft,
  The boldest might desire in vain.

And so, methought, whilst England holds
  That Truth and Right are first and best,
No daring hand shall ever pluck
  The flower of honour from her breast.

My husband took great interest in African explorations, in reading of Stanley's wanderings on the " Dark Continent," and of his *rencontre* with Livingstone. After the death of that dauntless pioneer he wrote the following :—

DIRGE ON THE BURIAL OF LIVINGSTONE IN WESTMINSTER ABBEY.

Bring home the dead !
Hark ! a host's tread !
Bow low each head !
    No pomp there needs
    No plume-crowned steeds,
    When each heart bleeds.
        Honoured of men !—
        But dust again !—
        Sound the knell, Ben !*

Find him a tomb
Mid minster gloom
Till day of doom !
    True hero guest
    He shall sleep best
    Where the great rest !
        Honoured of men !—
        But dust again !—
        Sound the knell, Ben !

His sun has set !
Passed is life's fret !
Nought to regret !
    His work is done !
    His race is run !
    His crown is won !
        Honoured of men !—
        But dust again !—
        Sound the knell, Ben !

---

* " Big Ben " is the great bell in the clock-tower at Westminster.

Through realms of night,
Where lions fight,
He let in light !
    He cleft a way
    Through beasts of prey
    For Gospel day !
        Honoured of men !—
        But dust again !—
        Sound the knell, Ben !

Not once hope-crushed
Till death pulse hushed
And heaven's joy flushed !
    Died at his post !
    Scorning life's cost !
    Lone, but not lost !
        Honoured of men !—
        But dust again !—
        Sound the knell, Ben !

Not for a name :
Not for mere fame :
But a grand aim !
    High aim and pure
    Crown to ensure
    Is to endure !
        Honoured of men !—
        But dust again !—
        Sound the knell, Ben !

CHAPTER XIV.

Illness of his son—Extract from an unpublished poem by J. R.
Withers—Failing health—Three Hymns : " Thy King-
dom come," " Psalm 137," " Father! who art in Heaven "
—His death—His funeral — Tributary verses by Dr.
Spencer T. Hall, and James R. Withers.

A CLOSE trial attended our lot in the serious illness of our young son from scarlet fever, during a
stay at Bristol in 1876; hovering as between life and
death, surely it was in answer to our prayers, and to
the vow breathed in the inmost heart, that he was
raised up again.

During his residence at Lexden my husband carried on a considerable correspondence with literary
people, and enjoyed at times their society in his own
home.

One of these was the rustic poet, James R. Withers,
of Cambridgeshire, who has written a pretty description of a visit he paid us, which I will venture to
quote from one of his unpublished poems :—

> " Near on a hill a town there stands
>   Built, as they say, by Roman hands;
>   And relics of that mighty race
>   Are thickly found around the place;
>   An ancient castle, grim and grey,
>   And ruins, grand in their decay,

Strong walls and gates long batter'd down,
When "Ironsides" besieged the town,
Of which some vestiges remain—
Such times we trust come not again.
Yet here are trained those sons of Mars
Whose trade and talk are guns and wars.
Oh! when shall all these horrors cease,
And men join hands in love and peace!
I heard the bugle call to drill,
The thundering drum, and clarion shrill;
I sigh'd, and could no longer stay,
By martial music scared away.
I left the town a mile behind
And then it was my hap to find
A quiet home beside the Colne,
Where Love has fixed his constant throne.
A peaceful calm pervades the place,
And tastes refined the mansion grace;
Around the trees lift high their heads,
Enclosing lawns and flowery beds,
Tall graceful trees, and all between
Are glossy laurels ever green,
And winding walks beneath the shade
That seem for musing poets made.
There is a little rustic seat,
From which I found it passing sweet
To gaze upon the vale below,
The mill, and river's peaceful flow;
While, just beyond, careering fast,
The "Iron horse" goes rushing past.
'Twas sweet to shut out noise and strife,
And all the anxious cares of life,
To watch the setting sun retire
Behind a bank of gold and fire,

And see the full-orb'd moon arise,
And yield to Fancy's witcheries ;
To hear the melancholy dove
Soft cooing in the neighbouring grove,
With harsher notes of pie or jay,
And see the nimble squirrels play,
While now and then an acorn brown
Or prickly chestnut thudded down.
And then to loiter by *that* pool,
Where crystal waters, fresh and cool,
In never failing plenty spring,
And through the meads the runnels sing.
O ! bless'd beyond the common lot
The dwellers in this charming spot.

    *   *   *   *   *

What can I wish for such a pair?
What bliss in which they do not share ?
I do not wish them greater wealth,
But strengthen'd and continued health.
And, since their sum of earthly joy
Is centred in their gentle boy,
That he may stand in brotherhood
Amongst the wise, the great, and good ;
I cannot wish a blessing higher
Than wishing all that they desire."

                     " Fairy Revels."

During the last few years of his life, my husband's health was very failing. A weakness of the heart occasioned him much trial. During 1880 he felt his powers too prostrate to care to go far from home, but paid what proved to be a last visit to some of his relatives at Kelvedon, and received many visits from friends at home. In the Eleventh Month of that year he was elected an alderman of the borough of Colchester. This was a gratifying tribute of respect to his long-tried worth ; but his health was very infirm, and he took but little part in the duties of his new office.

During the night of the 10th of Twelfth Month he had a severe attack of illness from which I doubted whether he would recover; but he rallied, and was permitted again to join the home circle, and to resume his usual quiet employments within doors, getting out but little during the winter.

I have given but occasional allusions to his inward religious feelings. He was not one to talk much of these ; but I believe there was a deep under-current of piety, and that there was an earnest endeavour to lead a consistent Christian life.

Some hymns, written by him, may here follow; the third is, as far as I know, the last of his poetical effusions.

HYMN.

Thy kingdom come ! Thy will be done !
   O everlasting Lord !
Awake ! arise ! all glorious Sun,
   And shed Thy beams abroad.

Unnumbered lands and isles afar,
   Lie wrapt in pagan gloom,
Oh, wheel on high Thy blazing car,
   And bid the desert bloom.

On earth's wide field a million flowers
  To drink thy glory thirst,
They wait to own thy vital powers,
  And forth in beauty burst.

Arise, O Lord ! put on Thy strength,
  And bless Thy servants' zeal,
Who ride the ocean's weary length
  High on the trembling keel.

The thunders roll, the lightnings flash
  ' Along the gloomy wave,
But though the billows o'er them dash
  They know that Thou canst save.

Far from their home and native land,
  Beneath a torrid sky ;
E'en while they grasp the Indian's hand,
  They know that Thou art nigh.

And e'en though death itself betide,
  They bow to Thy decree,
They know that Thou for them hast died
  And they can die for Thee.

O Lord! Thy glorious day reveal,
  The last and best of days !
When all the sons of men shall kneel,
  And shout one song of praise.

PSALM CXXXVII.

By the rivers of Babylon there we sat down
In a strange land, poor strangers oppress'd and o'er-
  thrown,
We hangĕd our harps on the boughs of the willows,
And wept o'er our woe to the sound of the billows ;

Yea we wept when we thought, O loved Zion, of thee,
And remembered the time when thy children were free.

For there they who subdued us and led us away,
Required of us sternly the musical lay,
And they who despoiled us required of us mirth,
Saying, " Sing us a song of the land of your birth."
But how can we sing the sweet anthems of Heaven,
When far from our country in chains we are driven ?

O Zion ! if e'er I forget thy glad hill,
May this right hand forget all its harp-sounding skill
And dumb be my tongue if to love thee I cease,
Home of my fathers, thou city of peace !
O Salem ! though strangers thy walls may destroy,
I still will prefer thee above my chief joy.

————

" FATHER! WHO ART IN HEAVEN."

Father! who art in Heaven, my God, my Guide,
My Strength, My Trust, my Hope, my Life, my Light,
Humbly I seek to worship Thee aright
In spirit and in truth—in Thee abide—
Leaving the length, and breadth, and depth, and height,
Of Thy supernal ways, which Thou dost hide,
In Heavenly wisdom, from man's craving sight.
I thank thee for existence, though allied
To sin and death, for Christ, Thy Son, has died
Triumphant over both in Hell's despite ;
In whom, believing, I am sanctified,
And made His fellow-heir of glory bright ;
And when He comes in majesty and might
I shall be ever with Him at His side.

Some weeks before the close, on my inquiring
as to whether, if the call came suddenly, he felt
prepared, he assured me of his firm reliance upon
the Rock Christ Jesus.

The call did come suddenly.

On the 23rd of Second Month, 1881, he attended
the week-day religious meeting of Friends in Colchester, and on the 25th walked in his garden
and planted a tree, remarking, however, to his
gardener, " Perhaps this may be the last I shall
ever plant."

He retired to rest at about his usual hour, bright
and cheerful, but in the course of the night was
taken ill, and, though various means were tried for
his relief, he passed away, in about an hour, on the
26th of Second Month, 1881, in the seventy-third
year of his age.

Yes thou art gone ! the strife is o'er !
   The "light afflictions " all are past !
Though here they tried thy spirit sore,
   How light to thee they seem at last.
Farewell, my precious one, farewell !
How dear thou wast words fail to tell.

I sometimes think thou still art near,
   Though closely veiled from mortal eyes,
Permitted still my path to cheer,
   To soothe me when the billows rise,
I seem to see thy well-known face
Beaming with love and heavenly grace.

No cloud upon thy spirit now,
  No anxious thoughts to press thee down,
A "weight of glory" on thy brow,
  And thine a never-fading crown,
Eternal joy and perfect rest,
How blest thou art, for ever blest !

Oh, be it mine to follow still
  Thy footsteps in the narrow way,
Bowing to all the Father's will,
  Thy God my God, thy Strength my Stay;
Till, on that bright and blissful shore,
We may unite to part no more !

And our loved child, our youthful son,
  Fair offshoot from the aged tree,
May he his course in wisdom run,
  Be all his God would have him be;
Bring honour to the name he bears,
Raise many a heart from crushing cares.

Fair is the picture Love would trace
  For that young precious life to be,
Bright with true love and every grace,
  From Folly's gilded thraldom free;
And, when his earthly course is run
His, too, the welcome words, " Well done."

The funeral, on the 4th of Third Month, was
largely attended, and proved a solemn occasion. In
the meeting words of exhortation were addressed from
the text, " Be ye also ready, for at such an hour as
ye think not the Son of Man cometh." I believe
that many who followed him to his last resting-place
felt that they had lost a true friend.

Some tributary verses may fittingly close this memoir :—

So rests his wearied frame in native earth,
But ne'er can be entombed his wit and worth;
Long in his cheery volumes they will shine :
And find in many a heart a living shrine:
Nay more, his spirit, in the realms above,
Where all is holiest intellect and love,
Will be at home, and God Himself adore,
When fame is dead and "time shall be no more."

DR. SPENCER T. HALL.

"IN MEMORY OF MR. JAMES HURNARD."

Gathered like golden grain when fully ripe,
　And safely garnered in the upper skies,
His mourning 's ended, for his God shall wipe
　All dimming tears for ever from his eyes.

How clearly must his raptured spirit trace
　The beauties of that glorious world above—
Know all the mysteries of sustaining grace,
　And all the wonders of redeeming love.

Freed from earth's thrall that clogs the spirit here,
　No taint pollutes his spotless robes of white,
Made meet in that Assembly to appear,
　Companion of the " firstborn sons of light."

Our selfish hearts would here have held him yet—
　The widow and the orphan sadly sigh ;
And age and want remember with regret
　His ready helping hand and sympathy.

A few short years were only mine to know
  His kindred spirit and his sterling worth,
To see the " setting sun's " resplendent glow,
  That now has " set " indeed from this our earth.

But this our loss is his eternal gain,
  His warfare ended he has won the crown,
With the redeemed in bliss with Christ to reign,
  Where all is day, their "sun" no more goes down.

The Muses favoured him, and he was bold
  In praise of virtue, and in lashing wrong—
But now he's singing to his harp of gold
  A higher theme, that new and wondrous song.

In works of charity his life was spent,
  Did good by stealth and "blushed to find it fame;"
But these shall be his lasting monument,
  And grateful memories will embalm his name.

But higher praise he ever kept in view,
  And this his welcome and his great reward—
" Well done, thou faithful servant, good and true,
"Enter the joyful presence of thy Lord."

JAMES R. WITHERS.

www.ingramcontent.com/pod-product-compliance
Lightning Source LLC
Chambersburg PA
CBHW030132030726
47498CB00007B/2671